Chips, Beans and Limousines

by Leila Rasheed

USBORNE

The Fantastic Diary of Bathsheba Clarice de Trop

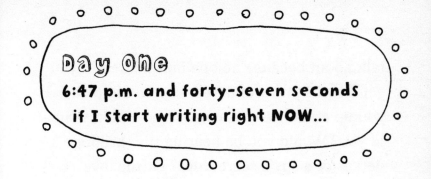

Day One
6:47 p.m. and forty-seven seconds
if I start writing right NOW...

Dear new Diary,

I have a surprise for you. It is a BIG
surprise. (Don't worry – it's also a GOOD
surprise!)

You are going to be so thrilled when I
tell you!!!

Are you sitting down???

...No, you are lying flat on my desk while
I write in you. Obviously. Okay, just breathe
deeply, and try to stay calm.

Dear Diary,

I can just imagine what your life was like on
the shelf at Paperflo's. Pretty dull, no?? No
one to talk to except other diaries. Nothing to

talk about because no one had written in you yet. Maybe you wondered who would pick you up and take you home. Who would write in you? Would you be hearing the thrilling details of a spy's secret life?? Or the love confessions of a wacky teenager??? Or the rotten poetry of a pimply computer geek????

Well. No. It's FAR more exciting than that!

Because – the hand that picked you up and took you home was MINE. The hand that is writing in you now, belongs to...

(I hope you are remembering to breathe deeply and stay calm...)

BATHSHEBA CLARICE DE TROP!!!!!!!!!!!!!!!!!!!

Ta Daaaaaaaah!!

Yes!! Yes yes yes yes yes yes yes yes yes!!!!!! THE Bathsheba Clarice de Trop!!!

You never thought you would belong to a celebrity, did you?

Yes. It is I. Heroine of *Bathsheba's Amazing Party*, *Bathsheba's Fabulous Friends*, *Bathsheba Saves the Day*, *Bathsheba Glamor Queen and the Smugglers of Doom* and *Bathsheba Shops* (vols. 1, 2 and 3). And all those other amazing, astonishing, best-selling a million times over books which my mother – the charming, beautiful and intelligent Mandy de Trop – writes about ME.

Me me me me me me me me me me me me!!!

Isn't it exciting?
Aren't you thrilled??
You are SO LUCKY!!!
You are going to be hearing ALL ABOUT ME!!!!

And we can be best friends, right?
Because that's what a diary is, isn't it?
A Girl's Best Friend.

No. Don't thank me. I know it's an honor for you, but after all, I'm just like you, really. Only FAMOUS!!!!!!!!!!!!!!!!!!
(And less papery.)

Ooo, there is Natasha, the housekeeper, calling me for dinner. I wish she would not call me "Bath," though. I must have a Word with her, like Mother does.

Mother isn't home yet.

I keep running out on to the landing because I think I hear the front door opening and it might be her, but it is always just Natasha bashing pans in the kitchen.

She might still get home in time for dinner. I do hope so!

Mother is so extraordinarily busy writing about me that sometimes I don't see her for *ages*. Sigh.

9:08 p.m. and sixteen seconds-ish.

No Mother, as usual. And Natasha had lots of work to do, so I had dinner by myself. I ate my lasagna in front of the television in the small living room with lots of cushions around me like a family. But even a small room can feel awfully big and empty when it is just you and *Doctor Who* in it.

I had a Word with Natasha. I said, "Natasha, maybe when you call me for dinner, instead of shouting 'Bath, dinner's ready,' you could shout 'Bathsheba Clarice de Trop, dinner's ready'."

Natasha laughed and laughed in a very disrespectful way, and said, "Bath, love, if I did that you'd never get any dinner. I'd be too busy saying your crazy name to cook anything."

I do not have a crazy name! Although I

suppose it is a little difficult to say. Bath-Shee-Ba. Cla-rees. (It's French!) Der Troe, like toe. (It's aristocratic!) Maybe you could repeat it after me, dear Diary, or maybe not, as I have just remembered you do not have a mouth.

Anyway, Bathsheba is a name for a Heroine! And a Movie Star, which is what I am going to be when I grow up. It is glamorous and dignified, unlike Bath. I mean, she might as well call me Shower Curtain and be done with it.

I pointed this out to her, but she just said, "Hurry up and eat your dinner, Butterball."

I wish she would not call me Butterball, either.

It makes me sound dumpy, which I am NOT. Very.

Oh, but I am so glad you are here, dear Diary!!! It will all be better now that I have someone to talk to. I mean, write in. Sometimes it does get a little dull being by myself. This evening, for example, I was so bored I tried to help Natasha make the lasagna, but she said "No chance, Bath, don't you remember what happened last time? I don't want another visit from the fire department!"

I don't think that is fair: anyone could mix up minutes and hours in a recipe. It is not my fault the canned tomatoes burst into flames.

Anyway, while I was eating my dinner, it struck me, dear Diary, that, being a book, and having lived on a Deprived Shelf all your life, you may not actually have read many other books.

And therefore it is possible – just possible – that you may not know all about me already.

Although probably you will have caught a glimpse of the novelty key rings, or the bookmarks, or seen other, not-famous girls, with their *Bathsheba – The Best by Far!* T-shirts. (Aren't they great? I've got twelve!)

Maybe I had better fill you in on what you've been missing. (Don't worry. The books are available, priced $8.99, from all good bookstores. You could ask for a boxed set for Christmas. There is still time to learn ALL ABOUT ME!!!)

Where shall I start?

Well, I am just always either
1) saving the day
or
2) having extraordinarily glamorous sleepovers with my amazing best friends, Aurelia Windsor-Battenberg and Fifi LaQuiche-Lorraine.

Aurelia and Fifi and me like to spend our time shopping at Harrods or Saks Fifth Avenue (if we are in America) or Gucci or Pucci or Prada.

Aurelia has smooth chestnut hair and is very refined and intelligent. She wears glasses but they are such expensive ones that she looks even better when she's wearing them than when she's not. She is fifteenth in line to the throne. Fifi has curly black hair and is extremely French and also a champion showjumper. Her mother is a supermodel and her father is related to the Prince of Monaco.

You are probably wondering why I am complaining about being bored when I could be out shopping or drinking lattes with my super-amazing friends, and, um, that is a really good question. The thing is, Aurelia and Fifi both have the measles, or possibly something more glamorous, so sadly they cannot be with us today. I know it is a really big coincidence that they have both got it at the same time, but things like that sometimes happen, and it does NOT mean it is not true.

Well, anyway, I do not have measles, and I

am just more glamorous and intelligent and champion-showjumper-y than either Fifi or Aurelia, and, also, I have Natural Leadership Skills. Plus, I have blonde hair, which is just the color of champagne, and is beautifully wavy, NOT frizzy.

Aurelia and Fifi and me go to a very select boarding school called St. Barnaby's. I just love boarding school! I am head of all the school, even though I am only in middle school (if you want to know why, read *Bathsheba's Victory*). And I am captain of the hockey team (*Hail, Bathsheba*) and of the swimming team and the riding team, and I am also house librarian and line monitor and more or less everything else too. Plus, I always star in all the plays our drama club puts on. I am top of my class in everything, including cooking, where my lasagna is always the best. I am just soooo good at everything that it is actually a little embarrassing sometimes!!!

But right now I am not at boarding school. It is the start of the summer vacation. As it is summer vacation, I expect I will have an adventure soon. I have saved the world thirteen times (*Bathsheba Crime-Fighter*, *Bathsheba Leads The Way*, *Bathsheba Triumphant*, *Bathsheba the Fabulous* and lots and lots of other books). I have also:

☆ Foiled a smugglers' plot (*Bathsheba on the Beach*)
☆ Discovered hidden jewels in an old farmhouse (*Bathsheba at Strawberry Fields Farm*)
☆ Driven off pirates (*Bathsheba's Caribbean Crisis*)
☆ Solved the murder of a catwalk model (*Bathsheba's Paris Plot*)
☆ Prevented a prize pony from being pony-napped (*Bathsheba's Pony Crisis*)

At the end of my adventures I always make a joke that everybody laughs at, even the bad guys, whom I have tied to chairs. And then my boyfriend, Brad, picks me up in his sky-blue Ferrari, and we drive off to the opera, or the beach, or a fashion show, or something else equally fabulous.

Oh yes, dear Diary! I have a boyfriend!!

Blush blush blush blush blush blush blush!!!

He is tall and handsome, and he has dreamy green eyes and a permanent suntan. He is sixteen and he can already drive, because he is American. He is a champion surfer and also a member of Mensa. He gives me diamond rings all the time because his father is a zillionaire computer genius and also descended from royalty.

So obviously, it's AMAZING being me!!!

Really!!!

Whenever it starts feeling as if Mother has not been home for a whole week or maybe two, I just think as hard as I can: *I am Bathsheba Clarice de Trop! My life is FANTASTIC!!!!!*

And it works. Usually.

I live in a PALATIAL MANSION with my mother. There is a darling old housekeeper called Ma Dovey who adores me and is just always baking me homemade cakes and cookies.

(Yes, I know I said Natasha was the housekeeper. Ma Dovey is sort of somewhere else at the moment... Maybe she has measles too.)

I have a massive swimming pool with my logo (I have a logo – it's a diamond-encrusted "B") set into the tiles at the bottom. I have seven walk-in closets (although I could have

lots more if I wanted), because there are only
seven colors I like to wear. They are

1) Hot Pink
2) Bright Blue
3) Green
4) Gamboge
5) Ecru
6) Vermilion
7) Mauve

I have two dressing tables with identical boxed
sets of makeup and jewelry, in case a friend
wants to come over and play. One of them
hasn't even been touched yet. Which is a
GOOD thing, and does not make me sad AT
ALL. Who wants other people messing up your
stuff anyway?

My bedroom has a carpet that is thick and pink and like walking through a forest, and a four-poster bed with a canopy with silk roses sewn onto it, and a life-size dollhouse (I'm a little old for it now, of course!)

And I have new skis!!

And I have two ponies!!!

And I have a jacuzzi!!!!

So there!!!!!

My life is FANTASTIC.

It's better than yours.

I'm going to bed now.

P.S. Goodnight, dear Diary, I really hope we can be friends. It can get lonely in the summer while waiting for an adventure to start.

o   o   o   o   o   o   o   o   o

Day Two

Just after lunch. (Caviar and lettuce pie! My favorite!)

Hello, dear Diary!

I hope you are settling in well. Do you like your shelf?

You are in select company.

You are sharing the shelf with the ENTIRE BOXED SET COLLECTION (special edition, gilded pages and red binding) of BATHSHEBA BOOKS!!!

You must be so pleased!

Anyway, today I am going to rehearse my next role.

St. Barnaby's drama club is putting on a new play. I am the star! Obviously.

I am A Little Princess from the book of the

same name, adapted into a play by Moi, Me, Bathsheba Clarice de Trop.

In case you don't know, it is all about this girl who is at a miserable, horrible school with a miserable, horrible teacher. Blerrgh! Her father dies so she has no money, and they make her live in an attic in the cold all alone. Everyone is horrible to her. But she wins them over by showing she is Angelic and Sweet-natured and A Little Princesscular. (Just like me!) And in the end she discovers she has a guardian, and lots of money. And her guardian (who is like a father) comes and takes her away from the horrible school and they live happily ever after.

My father is Not On The Scene.

Mother raised me alone, struggling against Adversity. (I think adversity means bad publicity. In fact, I am sure of it!)

Mother does not talk about my father, but I

expect he is probably very rich and glamorous. Maybe he is a Hollywood actor, who has to keep his love child (me!) secret. Or perhaps he is a top spy who has to maintain anonymity.

Yes, that is probably why he can't come and see me.

La la la la la la la la.

I don't mind!! My life is fabulous!!!

Did I say I had two ponies???

Showtime!

Now I am going to rehearse. If I prop you up here, dear Diary, you can watch. And applaud!

(Well, just rustle your pages, then.)

First I have to put on my costume. This is a

beautiful silk evening gown and high heels.
But a little disheveled, as it would be if you
lived in an attic.

Hmm.

It might look better if I was taller.

These are my lines:

A Little Princess –
*When things are horrible – just horrible –
I think as hard as ever I can of being a
princess. I say to myself, "I am a princess,
and I am a fairy one, and because I am
a fairy nothing can hurt me or
make me uncomfortable."*

Did you like it?

The part where I swooned on the sofa was particularly good, wasn't it?

I can't wait till Mother gets home. Maybe she will have time to watch me act. Oh, I hope so! Maybe tonight she won't be busy again!!!

I know she has a very important job (writing about me!) but I really, really wish she had time to watch me act. At this rate I will be grown-up before she sees me onstage, and I do not think I will make such a convincing Little Princess when I am sixteen or even older.

Later still.

Mother's not home yet. She is probably really busy writing. Or at a glamorous party with Agents.

I am so not dumpy...not with the light off, anyway.

Later, much later.

Still no Mother. The high heels are getting uncomfortable. But when I am a Movie Star I will have to wear them all the time, so I suppose I had better practice.

Later, later, later...

At last!! I can hear her in the hall!!!
   Back soon, dear Diary! Best friend!!
Mwah!!!

P.S. I just kissed a diary. Maybe that's a little weird.

Even later.   *

WELL.

Dear Diary,

You will not BELIEVE what happened.

I rushed downstairs.

"Mother, I am A Little Princess," I told her. "Do you want to see me act?"

"No time, dear, I'm afraid. Busy busy busy. Got to get organizing our Hutchford's Book Signing And Bathsheba Bash! Give me a kiss – no, just an air kiss, you'll spoil my makeup."

And she went into her study and shut the door.

I don't ever get sad, because my life is fantastic, but sometimes I feel as if I don't know what to do or where to go. I hate that feeling! It's like being hungry but eating doesn't fill it up. (I tried and it just gave me a stomachache.)

I sat on the stairs and recited my lines quietly to myself, but it was not the same.

Then I remembered. Natasha was still here. *She* would like to see me act!

"Natasha! I'm going to perform a show for you! *A Little Princess* – from the book of the same name. Adapted by—"

"I'm sorry, Bath. I'm in such a hurry. I have to get off on time tonight." She was rushing around the kitchen, with a can of tomatoes in one hand and a jar of herbs in the other.

"Oh, don't be silly! What are you in a hurry for? I'm going to entertain you!" I pulled out a chair for her.

"I'm going to see my goddaughter. In her school play."

Goddaughter??

Play???

"But this is FAR better," I said. "Besides, I have Genuine Talent."

She sort of rolled her eyes.

"Butterball, I'm late. Can't your mother watch you?"

"She's busy again."

"Oh." She looked kind of sorry, and then she said, "Maybe tomorrow, okay? I really have to get the cooking done now." And she pushed past me to get to the stove, which is not a housekeeperly thing to do!!

I was really angry.

"You are a rotten housekeeper," I shouted. "I am going to get Mother to bring Ma Dovey back!"

Diary, do you know what she did?

She looked at me and said: "Bathsheba, Ma Dovey is *fic-tion-al*."

I *hate* it when Natasha says things like that – it makes me feel stupid.

I was even more angry then. I said: "I suppose next you'll be telling me I'm fictional too!"

And do you know what she said?

She sighed and she said: "Well, actually, Bathsheba, yes, mostly you do seem to be."

And then she pushed me out of the kitchen!!

And shut the door in my face!!!

I don't know what she is talking about.

I am not fictional!

I am right here!

I don't believe she even really has a goddaughter. She certainly hasn't mentioned her before.

A little later.

What's so special about this stupid goddaughter anyway?

I bet I can act much better than her.

I can Emote. (I am not really sure what that means, but Mother says all the best actresses do it, so I suppose I do too.)

I bet this so-called goddaughter never
Foiled Smugglers.

A little little later. ✳

Maybe Emote means "Swoon on the Sofa"?
　　I can't imagine Natasha having a
goddaughter. I wonder if she calls her
Butterball too?
　　I sort of hope not.

A little little little later.

Dear Diary,
I have had the most astoundelicious idea!
　　Yes yes yes yes yes yes yes yes yes!!
　　I am soooooooooo amazing!!!
　　I am going to spy on Natasha!
　　I am going to wait until she leaves and then

follow her and see where she really goes.
I don't believe she has a goddaughter at all.
Certainly not one who can act! I bet she is
really smuggling emeralds, maybe in
packages of pasta. Or dealing in stolen
antiquities.

Ooooo, I will have to get disguised!!

It will be just like *Bathsheba in Havana*,
when I had to dress up as a vacuum cleaner
in order to be smuggled into an evil
mastermind's headquarters!

(It was a pretty uncomfortable disguise,
let me tell you, dear Diary. Have you ever
tried to breathe through a vacuum cleaner
tube? Well, don't. Yuck, yuck, yuck.)

This disguise will be FAR more stylish
(not that it would be difficult to get less
stylish than being disguised as a Hoover.
I do not think *Bathsheba in Havana* was
one of Mother's best books.)

This is going to be sooo much fun!

o   o   o   o   o   o   o   o   o

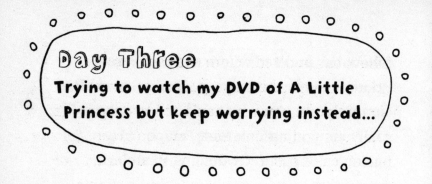

Day Three
Trying to watch my DVD of A Little Princess but keep worrying instead...

Dear Diary,

Huh, huh and double huh!

I am a little scared and worried. There is a secret going on. Mother is very stressed, and there is a stranger downstairs in her study. I peered over the banisters and whoever it is has a bald head, but I couldn't see anything else.

Mother told Natasha to take the day off. It feels funny, Natasha not being here and Mother being here, as it is usually the other way around.

Well, I don't care if Mother doesn't want to tell me what's going on. I have my Art. I mean my acting. I am practicing my lines again.

I have taken all the clothes out of my gamboge closet and hung them around like an audience. You are the Guest of Honor, dear Diary, as you are my Best Friend (except for Aurelia and Fifi, of course, who are sadly not here because they are ill with appendicitis, I think it was, or maybe they broke all their legs in a glamorous skiing accident).

Huh! St. Barnaby's production will be MUCH better than that garbage I saw last night... Ooh, dear Diary, I haven't told you what happened last night, yet, have I?

WELL.

It was extraordinary.

When I had decided to spy on Natasha, I put on very big dark glasses, and a very big hat (with vermilion flowers) and a very big feather boa (hot pink). I looked very distinguished – you could hardly see my freckles at all and the pink and vermilion were so exciting that I thought nobody would

 33 ☆

ever notice my hair. (Sometimes my hair can look a little more mousy than beautiful blonde, which is really annoying. It is probably all down to the wrong shampoo, because really my hair *should* be blonde, and shouldn't stick out sideways either, the way it sometimes does.) Anyway, I knew I had to disguise myself really well, because after all, I am famous. Then I had a fabtastic idea! As everybody knows, I only wear seven colors. So, to be really disguised, I would wear a totally different color!

I went into Mother's bedroom, which is all white, and went into her big mirrored closet, and got out her white suit. The skirt was a little long, but the jacket fit quite well.

No one would ever recognize me!

Then I called a taxi on my cell phone. I had some allowance left over from last time Mother gave me some. So I put that in my handbag.

"I want him to park on the other side of the street and not to honk the horn," I told the person on the other end of the line. "I will come out soon after six. Discretion is essential."

"Whatever, honey," she said helpfully.

A spy's plans cannot be too carefully laid.

I hid at the top of the stairs, where I could watch the front door. Just after six, Natasha came hurrying out of the kitchen, putting on her coat as she went.

"Goodnight," she called, as she closed the door behind her.

I waited for a minute, until I was sure she had gone. Then I hurried downstairs, and opened the door cautiously. Thankfully she was parked some way down the street, so she didn't see me as I scurried across the road and slunk into the taxi.

"Follow that car," I told the driver. "The blue Beetle. And make it snappy."

The driver did not appear to be in a hurry.

"Have you got any money, kid?"

"Well, *obviously*," I said irritably. Really, some people are stupid. "Or I wouldn't be getting in a taxi, would I?"

"All right, little madam," he said as he drove off. At least he had the manners to call me madam.

I peered excitedly through the window, watching Natasha's blue Beetle as it drove through the city. I expected she would head for the docks, or the airport, or at the absolute very least a deserted farmhouse.

But no!

She just kept on going. It was taking ages. I stopped being excited and started feeling worried about the meter. I didn't know it cost so much to go in a taxi.

Finally Natasha's car turned into the gates of a big, dark, ugly building, like an upturned shoebox.

At last! I thought.

The abandoned pasta warehouse!

But it wasn't.

A sign on the gate said *Welcome to Clotborough School.* A lot of people were going in through the doors, talking to each other noisily. It looked as if it actually *was* a school play. But it was very different from the plays we have at St. Barnaby's. At St. Barnaby's, all the mothers wear diamanté evening gloves, and all the fathers wear those suits that make you look like a penguin, and there is a special marquee to put the nannies in. These parents were just wearing jeans and ordinary stuff, and they did not look glamorous at all, but they did look comfortable. Which I suppose is important too.

I actually only just had enough money to pay the driver. I wondered how I was going to get home. There were a lot of boys and girls who were my age, hanging around and talking, or giggling and chasing each other.

I suddenly felt a little shy and nervous.

I am Famous! I reminded myself. *My life is Fantastic!! I am Bathsheba Clarice de Trop!!!*

"Are you getting out, honey, or what?" said the taxi driver.

So I got out. It looked too busy for a spy hideout. But I did not despair! It was quite possible Natasha could be meeting her accomplice during the intermission. Maybe there were code words hidden in the script!!

Two girls in green uniforms ran past me, screaming and giggling. They looked as if they were having a lot of fun. Just for a little moment, I wondered what it would be like to go to Clotborough School.

...It would be horrible. Obviously. Not fun at all.

I followed everyone else into the school, concentrating on looking inconspicuous. Some people still stared at me, though.

You'd think they had never seen a feather boa before. We went through into a big room with a stage at one end. The seats were just plastic, not red velvet like at St. Barnaby's. Still, it felt exciting. I could see the curtains billow as people moved around behind them. I edged into a seat. Obviously the play would be awful.

A very round, smiley lady squidged in next to me. As she settled her shawls and her handbag, she saw me looking at her and smiled even more.

"You must be on after the intermission! What a wonderful costume. And what part are you playing, dear?" she asked.

"A Little Princess," I said, without thinking. She laughed.

"Oh no, dear, you can't be. That's Keisha's role."

Then everybody started clapping, and the curtains opened and there she was!

A Little Princess!

Someone else playing MY role!!!

I gaped at her. I couldn't believe it.

She was standing in the middle of the stage, which looked like a Victorian drawing room. It even had a birdcage with some real birds in it. There was also a boy dressed like A Little Princess's father, and a girl with a sour face like the horrible teacher, but I couldn't stop looking at A Little Princess. She had curly black hair, and was wearing a gorgeous silk dress with a frill, but I didn't even notice that until later. And that was because her face looked exactly as if she had just been told that her father was going away for a long, long time – and she was trying really hard not to feel as if she didn't know what to do or where to go. Even though she looked so unhappy, she looked really nice – like the kind of person you would want to be your best friend.

NO!!!!!!!!!!!!!!

Dear Diary, what am I saying?

I already have TWO best friends, who completely admire me and always want to do exactly what I tell them to!!!

Is this girl a champion showjumper????

I don't think so!!!!!

I bet she has never even been on a pony. (Of which I have two.)

I bet she is not nearly royal, or French. And she is probably not intelligent or refined!!!

So I totally don't care. And even though at the time, I admit, I thought she was quite a good actress, I bet she really can't act and it was just pretending, and not Natural Talent (of which I have lots).

Anyway, while the play was going on, I forgot totally to keep an eye out for spies, because it was really, really good. Oops, I mean bad.

At the intermission, I clapped really hard (just to blend in with the rest of the audience, obviously) and as we were getting up, the round lady bent over and said to me: "You were quite enthralled, weren't you! I think you must know the lines by heart – I could see your lips moving."

I smiled at her.

"Yes, I have a creative, artistic soul," I told her. "I am an actress myself, after all."

I went out into the hall, where people were milling around, eating potato chips and drinking orange juice. And right there was Natasha!

She was talking to the girl who played A Little Princess!!

Obviously there *were* code words in the script after all!!!

I pulled my hat down really low, and wrapped

my boa up tight so it covered half my face.
Then I crept up close so I could hear what
they were saying.

"It's really cool you could come, Aunty
Tash," the girl was saying.

"Well, I wasn't going to miss your starring
role, was I, Keisha? Mind you, I nearly did – I
had a tough time getting out of work today."

"Why, what happened?"

"Oh, just Bathsheba again. It's not fair to
talk behind Mrs. de Trop's back. But I will say
this, I feel really sorry for her poor kid. Even
though she is a brat."

Brat??

Sorry for me???

Dear Diary, I was furious!!
  I couldn't believe it!!!
  My life is FANTASTIC!!!!!!!!
  (*Two* ponies!!)
  How *rude* of her!!!

I forgot all about being in disguise.

"You are horrible," I told Natasha at the top of my voice. "First you say I'm fictional. Then you say I'm a brat. And you're sorry for me. Huh! Well, actually my life is FABULOUS!!! You don't have to feel sorry for me at all. Actually, you should feel jealous!!!!!"

Keisha was staring at me with her mouth wide open, as well she might, for she had probably never met a celebrity before.

"I," I told her, "have two ponies. And a boyfriend. And seven walk-in closets. And I bet you haven't got any of those things. My life is FANTASTIC!!!! How dare you feel sorry for me!!!!!"

"Bathsheba!"

I'd never seen Natasha look so angry. Suddenly I realized everyone was staring at me. And not in a "Wow, look, a celebrity" sort of way. I quickly pulled off my hat and glasses so they would recognize me. But instead they kept on staring, really quite embarrassingly. I felt almost like crying, but I made myself not, because I definitely didn't want anyone to feel sorry for me AT ALL.

"What are you doing here?" hissed Natasha.

"You're *Bathsheba*?" said Keisha. "But I thought she had champagne blonde hair, and was really slim and gorgeous. That's what it says in the books. Your hair is more...sort of mousy. And you're too short to be Bathsheba. I don't mean that in a bad way," she added hurriedly. "This isn't really Bathsheba Clarice de Trop, is it, Aunty Tash?"

"Oh, don't you start!" exclaimed Natasha, before I could say anything at all. "Bathsheba in the books is a made-up character! Mrs. de Trop just writes stories about someone with her daughter's name, that's all! It's pretend."

WELL!!!!!!!

I opened my mouth, but Natasha turned around and grabbed me by the arm.

"Is your mother with you?" she demanded. "Does she know you're here?"

I actually felt a little scared. She looked really, really angry. Even angrier than me. I shook my head.

"This is the last straw!" said Natasha. "I have absolutely had enough! It's bad enough to be underpaid and overworked, but your behavior is just too much! I am giving in my notice tomorrow."

I opened my mouth, but I couldn't say anything. I really, really didn't want Natasha to leave. She's the only person who sometimes talks to me. Even if she does keep telling me I'm fictional, which is NOT TRUE.

"Keisha, I'm sorry. I have to go. I have to take this silly little girl home at once."

"But you'll miss the rest of the play!" Keisha looked really upset.

"Yes, well, you know who to blame for that!" Natasha glared at me.

"Please, can't you both just stay till the end?" said Keisha, looking at me. "It's only another half hour."

"Oh, please," I said. I don't know why. It just slipped out.

"Well," said Natasha after a moment. "I suppose your mother is probably not panicking about you."

"Oh no," I said hastily. "She didn't even notice I'd gone."

Natasha sighed.

"Typical. Well, okay then. But take that ridiculous feather boa off. You look like a pantomime dame."

In the car on the way home, Natasha was very quiet. I was feeling really worried.

"Natasha?"

"What is it now?"

"Are you really going to leave? Because I'll really miss you – and your lasagna."

She was quiet for a minute, and then she said, "Hah. No. I need the money. But I am going to have a very serious talk with your mother."

As we went up to the door, Natasha took out her key. But just as she was going to put it into the lock, Mother opened the door instead.

"Mrs. de Trop," Natasha started, "I'm sorry, but this is not my fault."

But Mother didn't even look surprised to see me outside. She looked...flustered. Mother never looks flustered. She wasn't wearing any makeup. Mother always puts on makeup to answer the door. She pushed a hand distractedly through her hair. I'd never even seen her touch her hair before – usually it is all blonde and smooth and beautifully calm as if she has cast a spell on it or something. But when she took her hand away I could see all her roots, which are the same color as my hair.

And she looked just like me when I'm really worried about something, like missing the last episode of *Hollywood Hopefuls*. Except worse. A lot worse. Natasha seemed to realize something was wrong, because she stopped and said "Mrs. de Trop, are you all right?"

"Yes. Er – yes. Natasha – could we talk tomorrow? Tonight is a little – complicated. In fact – not tomorrow. I'd prefer that you didn't come in tomorrow. Take a day off. I'll pay you, of course."

Natasha gaped at her, and then glanced at me, but I didn't know what was going on either.

Mother took my hand. She never takes my hand. I was really scared. I knew something had gone horribly wrong, or else I was in really big trouble.

"Mother? What's wrong?" I asked, as she shut the door on Natasha.

"Wrong? Nothing. I've just had an...

unexpected phone call." She frowned at me, and her voice sounded slightly more normal, as she said, "Bathsheba, what were you doing outside? And why are you wearing my best suit?"

It was quite difficult to explain, dear Diary, let me tell you. But the really scary thing is, she didn't even get angry. She just nodded absentmindedly, and then sent me off to bed.

So now I am dying to know what is going on, and why someone is in Mother's study.

I tried listening at the door with a glass like I did in *Bathsheba's Paris Plot*, but all I can hear is sounds like whales singing or something, which is unlikely as there is no water in there.

I have been trying to practice my lines, but every time I start saying them, I keep wondering what is going on downstairs. Or else thinking about that Keisha girl from last night who was being A Little Princess on a real stage with a real audience. I wonder how she managed to look like that. Like she knew what it felt like to have your dad go away forever.

Huh, I can't believe she said I didn't look like myself.

I am looking in the mirror right now, and, okay, maybe I am not as tall as I thought I was. I am champagne blonde though! Well, kind of. Sort of. It depends on the sort of champagne. Mousy brown champagne... If I close the curtains and squint it looks better...

I wonder if I can make my face go the way Keisha's did when she was acting?

Not that she was any good, obviously.

...Ooh, Mother is calling me.

Finally, dear Diary, I get to find out what's going on!

o o o o o o o o o

Day Four

Dear Diary,

I do not really know where to start.

I have had the most awful experience.

I feel a little funny, and dear Diary, I know you are my best friend, but I really, really wish I had a friend who could talk. I could call her up, or if she lived near she could come over, and I could tell her about my awful evening, and she would not get annoyed or be busy, but she would listen, and maybe then I would feel better about everything. Maybe if Fifi were here, or Aurelia, or Brad, I could tell them. But somehow I cannot imagine them being much help. I don't know if they would understand. Because things are usually perfect for them. Not horrible and complicated, like now.

They might laugh.

I have looked through some of my books and no, nothing like this has ever happened to me before.

When Mother called me I went rushing downstairs really quickly. But I stopped running when I saw Mother's face.

"Oh, Bathsheba," she said. "Can you – er – can you come into the study, please?"

I hardly ever go into Mother's study. I might get something dirty. There was someone sitting in one of Mother's white velvet chairs. A small, bald, worried-looking man, in patched jeans and a brown sweater that looked as if it had come from a thrift store. He stood up nervously as we came in, wiping his hands down his jeans as if they were sweaty. I wondered if he could be a lawyer. But he didn't look smart enough to be a lawyer. He looked normal. Ordinary. Like the parents at Clotborough School. The really weird thing was that I could tell he was really pleased to see me. His eyes were shining as if he had been given the most amazing present. And at the same time, he looked really nervous – as if he couldn't quite believe the present was for him, and he was scared it might be taken away any moment.

My mother sighed, and patted her forehead with a tissue.

"Bathsheba – this is your…well, your father."

???

YUCK!!

Dear Diary, I did not say this out loud, but I think it showed in my face, because the man blinked and stepped back. When he looked up again his eyes weren't pleased anymore, they were anxious. He smiled, but not a real smile, more the sort you do in the mirror to try and make yourself feel happy when you're not.

"Hello, Bathsheba!" he said.

It was a totally fake happy voice. I could tell it was fake because my voice does that too when I'm trying to sound confident and amazing but really I feel like crud. It goes all exclamation-marky.

"Mother," I said, "you are joking, right?"

"Obviously not, Bathsheba," she snapped. "Why on earth would I joke about something like – like this?"

She glanced at the man, and he glanced at her, and I knew, with a horrible feeling, as if I was slowly being filled full of cold rice pudding, that she meant it.

I moved around so the armchair was between me and the man. I could tell Mother was trying to behave as if everything was okay, but she looked just as confused and upset as I felt. I think she was thinking *Yuck* too. We both stood there staring at him, looking all brown and shabby in the middle of Mother's gorgeous white study. It felt as if someone had delivered a huge awkward package to our house by mistake and now we were stuck with it. Him.

The man looked back and forth between us.

"I suppose you haven't told Bathsheba anything about me," he said in a small, tight voice.

"Well, really. Why would I? It's not exactly the kind of thing one *boasts* about, Bill."

Bill!

Double yuck!!

What a totally unglamorous name!!!

"If you're my father, *Bill*," I said sarcastically, "where have you been? Why haven't you ever come to see me before? Huh?"

Bill turned, very slowly, red.

"I – maybe I can tell you tomorrow," he said. "It's a long story. But, Bath – I'm very sorry. I would have come if I could."

"My name's Bathsheba," I said. "Not Bath. Do you see scented bubbles coming out of my nose? No? Well, then."

He smiled.

"Sorry. It's just that Bath was my special name for you, when you were a baby."

When I was a baby?

"Oh," I said. "You mean you used to be around? And then you got bored and went away? Was that it?"

"No!" said Bill, and Mother said, "We did *try* to make it work. For a while."

"But you went away," I said. I felt as if I had a boiled egg stuck in my throat, and if I swallowed I'd choke or cry or something. "You didn't even write."

Bill sighed, and gave Mother a hard look. "I suppose you didn't pass on my letters, did you? I should have expected that."

"With *that* return address?" snapped

Mother. "Imagine how she would have felt!"

They stared at each other like two cats about to have a fight. I sort of sidled out from in between them, because for a minute I thought they might actually start really fighting, you know, like wrestlers on TV when they come bouncing off the ropes and headbutt each other in the tummy. But instead, Bill sighed, and looked at me.

"I thought about you lots, you know," he said. "I'm really, really sorry."

Yeah, RIGHT, I thought.

He kept staring at me, as if he wanted me to do something. I don't know what. The cancan? Look happy?

"Don't you remember," he said, "how we used to go for walks in the park? We fed the ducks and the geese and the squirrels. You liked the squirrels best. And then we got chips?"

"She was only little," retorted my mother. "Of course she doesn't remember. And Bathsheba never has chips. They are extremely unhealthy and fattening."

"Well, I remember," said Bill. He kept looking at me, and his brown eyes were suddenly warm, like he wanted to hug me. Only he didn't. Thankfully! "We had lots of fun together, you and me. We were best buddies. How about we go and do something like that tomorrow? Feed the ducks? Go to a café and get chips and beans? I've come here to see you, Bath – I mean Bathsheba. I'd really like us to get to know each other again. I'd like to be friends."

Yuck!!!

As if as if as if as if as if as if!!!

"I don't have to, Mother, do I?" I asked her.

Bill looked horribly disappointed. Mother glanced at him.

"Well..." she said, running her hand through her hair. "It might be a good idea, Bathsheba.

But right now – right *now*, Bill, I think you should go."

It was awful. I've never seen Mother look nervous before.

Bill nodded. He went awkwardly to the door. As he passed me, he made a sort of movement as if he was going to ruffle my hair, or touch my cheek, or something, but I backed away and stared at him until he turned red and changed the movement into scratching his ear instead.

"I'll come by at ten tomorrow," he said to Mother.

I didn't follow him into the hall. I held on to the back of Mother's white velvet chair, and when she came back into the study I knew she must be really stressed because she didn't even get on to me for touching her furniture with dirty hands.

"He's not really my father, is he?" I demanded.

"Yes, he is, I'm afraid."

I could see all the lines on her face. As if she was breaking up like a jigsaw puzzle. I really, really wanted her to tell me it was all a joke, or a mistake.

"Are you sure? I don't believe he is! I don't want to go with him! He could be anyone. He could be a kidnapper. Mother, you won't make me, will you?"

"Listen," she said hastily, sitting down, "whatever else he is, he's your father. I'm sorry, Bathsheba. But that's how it is. Of course, it's your choice, but I think you should go, tomorrow. It's just one day." She sighed and rubbed her forehead. "I suppose he deserves a chance. Really, I didn't think he'd come back."

I sat down on the carpet, behind the chair so she couldn't see my face. My mouth was wobbling and my eyes felt as if they were going to start crying without me.

"He did write," she said suddenly. "I'll give him that, he did write. Maybe I should have passed the letters on. But I was trying to protect you!"

I swallowed a couple of times.

"Where was he?" I asked. "Why didn't he ever come and see me before?"

"I can't tell you. He'll have to."

"But you *know*, don't you?" I could tell just from her voice.

"Yes. Look, Bathsheba, I think you had better go to bed now. I need some time alone."

I stood up and went slowly to the door. As I went out, she said quickly, "Bathsheba?"

"What?"

"He seemed quite different when I met him. A totally different person."

And, dear Diary, this is JUST what I was thinking. How could such a glamorous and charming and talented person like my mother, Mandy de Trop, Celebrity Authoress, possibly, possibly, possibly, end up with such a boring, shabby, BALD little man???

I mean!!!

Gruesome!!!!!

And dear Diary, I am not sure what to think anymore. It is really late, but I can't sleep.

WHY didn't he come to see me for years and years?

Maybe he is an astronaut, and was on a space mission to Mars??

Maybe he is a secret agent and was undercover in a foreign country???

Maybe he was doing top secret work on aliens for the government????

I suppose, *suppose*, there might be a good explanation.

I suppose he might be glamorous after all, and just hiding it very well. (This would make sense if he was a spy.)

Maybe the bald head is just a disguise!

But even if it is, I don't think he could ever be glamorous enough to make up for years and years of totally behaving as if I didn't exist.

It feels like I have swallowed a stone and now it's sitting in my stomach as if it was at the bottom of a cold, dark pond.

I wonder why he's come back now?

I suppose I will find out tomorrow. It might not be so bad after all. Maybe there is a very good reason why he could not come and see me.

But if he thinks I am going to like him, he has another think coming. Huh.

o   o   o   o   o   o   o   o   o

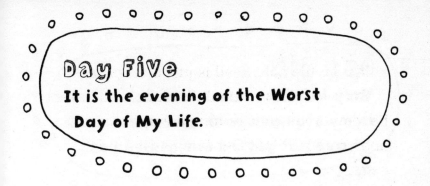

Day Five

It is the evening of the Worst Day of My Life.

Do not ask me what the time is.

I do not know.

I do not care.

What does it matter anyway? The day is Dark, and so is my Soul.

I wish I did not have a father, like A Little Princess.

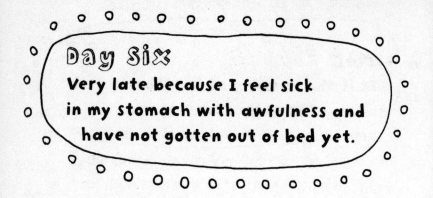

Day Six
Very late because I feel sick in my stomach with awfulness and have not gotten out of bed yet.

Dear Diary,
You know I said it might not be so bad after all?

Well, ha!

Ha ha ha ha ha ha ha ha ha ha ha ha ha ha.

And NOT in a funny way.

It is worse than bad.

It is TERRIBLE.

Oh oh oh oh oh oh oh oh oh oh oh.

Oh, dear Diary,
I am so ashamed. My life is RUINED.

I will never, never, never get out of bed again.

Later.

I had to get up to get a peanut-butter sandwich. Natasha looked at me funny because I was still in my pajamas, but she didn't ask any questions. Which is a good thing.

I can't tell ANYONE about this.

I am almost glad my friends are not here because they would all be laughing at me now and calling me names and not talking to me. If Brad knew he would just dump me immediately. And so would Fifi and Aurelia. I can just imagine how they would look at me down their noses, and snicker.

Maybe Keisha would not laugh.

**I still do not know the time.
I have no strength to look at
the clock as I am Frustrated
with Grief.**

Dear Diary,
This is definitely Adversity.

I will tell you what happened yesterday
as you are only a diary and won't tell anyone
and anyway I have to tell someone as I am
just fed up of it being in my head.

Bill arrived at nine-thirty, which was
early.

Early is sometimes good, and sometimes,
dear Diary, it is not. I still had the cold stone
in my stomach when I woke up. It made me
feel miserable all the time I was getting
dressed, and it left no room for breakfast
either.

It was still there when Bill arrived. I could

see he had tried to spruce himself up, but his suit was frayed at the cuffs and unpleasantly shiny. It was clearly not Gucci or Pucci or Prada.

Mother had called Natasha and told her not to come in until twelve. I think she was embarrassed too.

"Hello, Bathsheba," said Bill. "How are you this morning?"

I gave him a Look. I almost felt bad afterward, because his smile wavered and shrunk up and disappeared just as if it was a balloon and I'd let the air out. But then I reminded myself that he had not come to see me for *years*. And then just turned up, wanting to be friends!

At least, I thought, *it's only for one day. Then he'll go off somewhere else and I won't ever have to see him again.*

…Unless he turns out to be a secret agent in disguise!!!

He kept looking at me sideways as we walked down the street. I did not really know what to think. I was still hoping that at any moment we would be attacked by Peruvians wielding poison darts and it would turn out to be the start of my next adventure.

But he did not try to whisper any code words to me, and nobody tried to bundle us into the back of a van. All he did was waffle on about his memories.

"You've really grown," he said. "I mean, you know, obviously. But it's still a surprise. I remember pushing you in the stroller! And here you are, nearly grown-up!"

Nearly!!

Huh!!!

It felt a little funny, thinking of him being my dad, ages ago. I sort of wanted to ask him about it, like what color was the stroller, and what did we used to talk about, and so on. But I squashed the feeling up tight. He obviously didn't enjoy being my dad as much as he said he did, or he would have stuck around.

"Where's your car?" I asked.

"I don't have one."

I stared at him. He turned red.

"I thought we could walk," he said. "Take the bus. It's a nice day."

I sighed. *Boring*. Well, maybe he would take me shopping. Frankly, it was the least he could do.

I almost decided I was not going to talk to him anymore (unless the Peruvians attacked). But I couldn't help feeling curious. After all, he was my father.

He looked nothing like me. Well, maybe his eyes did. But I didn't like looking at his eyes. They just looked like big, pleading puppy eyes, and they made me feel guilty and upset.

"So what shall we do?" he asked. "How about the ice rink?"

I sniffed.

"I don't think so."

"Oh, can't you skate?"

"Of course I can skate! I'm top of my class at skating. Actually I was nearly picked to go in the Olympic ice-skating team but I had to pull out because the Prime Minister urgently needed my help to solve the Case of the Disappearing Archbishop!!!"

He gave me a funny sort of look.

"Um – when was this?"

"In *Bathsheba and the Dinosaurs from Mars*, of course. Are you telling me you haven't even bothered to read about me?"

"Oh yes. The books." He frowned. "Yes, your mother's done well with those, hasn't she? Good for her."

"I suppose so." I shrugged. "She is a fabulous writer, but of course, I am her inspiration. That's why we always do book signings together. Like the Bathsheba Bash, at Hutchford's Book Emporium on Piccadilly Circus."

"That sounds fun. Don't suppose I could come?"

"The tickets are seven-fifty each, from Hutchford's," I said frostily.

"Great! I'll get one tomorrow."

Some people do not know when they are not wanted.

"So – the ice rink?" he asked.

"No! I don't skate with just ordinary people! I only skate when I can have my own private ice rink. I don't think you realize how difficult it is being a celebrity. People are ALWAYS mobbing me."

It was a little annoying that the street happened to be completely empty just then (except for us, obviously).

"Well, how about a movie, then? You choose the show."

I was really tempted because I soooo want

to see *Fright Night,* and Mother is always too busy to take me. But I pulled myself together. There was absolutely no reason for me to forgive him at all.

"I only go to exclusive previews, when I walk down the red carpet with Brad."

"Brad?" He looked a little startled. "Who's Brad?"

"My boyfriend," I said airily. "He's sixteen—"

"*What?*"

"—and sometimes he helps me with solving mysteries, like the Paris Shows murder, or rescuing the president from being held for ransom by evil Bolivian guinea-pig smugglers."

"Oh." He relaxed a little. "This is all in the books, is it?"

"*Bathsheba's Paris Plot* and *Bathsheba and the Jaguar's Tail.* If you'd bothered to read the books, you'd know all about me and my amazing life. Look," I said, because I was feeling sorry for him as he obviously had Not a Clue, "I'll lend you my boxed set, all right? Then you can read them and find out what I'm really like."

He smiled.

"I want to get to know the real you, Bath. Not the book version!"

"Well, it's all *in* there," I said, feeling slightly miffed.

He sighed.

"It's funny how similar we are," he said, with a sort of sad smile.

Yuck!!!!!!!!!!!!!!

"We are not similar in the slightest," I retorted. "You, for a start, have far less hair."

He laughed.

"Yes, I'm definitely a baldy," he said cheerfully, just as if he didn't care what he looked like at all. "Look, what about the Natural History Museum?"

"Museum?"

"Yes, you know. The Natural History Museum. They have an amazing dinosaur skeleton. It's as big as a bus."

"Has it been stolen?" Perhaps this was where the adventure started.

"What? Not so far as I know."

I sighed.

"Look, Bill," I said. "I don't really do museums and ice rinks and stuff. If you'd read my books, you'd know that."

"Well, what do you do, then? When you're not saving the world, obviously."

"Shopping trips to exclusive boutiques. Beach parties. Sleepovers at the Ritz. Nail bars. Spas. Polo games. Glamorous hairdressers."

"Well," he said. He had turned slightly pink. "I'm afraid I can't take you on a shopping spree, and I don't have any hair to dress, so I suppose we'll just go to the park, then, shall we?"

"Fine," I shrugged.

I dragged along behind him with my head down and a look of deep contempt on my face, trying to look as little as possible like his daughter, because, honestly, he didn't deserve it.

I hadn't been to the park for ages. The squirrels actually are rather cute. They go bounding along with their tail curving behind them, like a row of mmmmmmmmmms, and then they make an r, when they sit up and eyeball you nervously, as if you might explode.

Bill took a packet of peanuts out of his pocket and crouched down and started tossing them to the squirrels. I watched them come right up to his hand and snatch a nut and then hurry off and sit there nibbling it and looking at him suspiciously as if they were worried he would try to get it back.

"Come on, Bath! It's fun!"

Obviously just to shut him up, I took a handful of peanuts and started chucking them at the squirrels.

"If you crouch down, they'll come closer," he told me.

"I *know*."

I sat down and tossed the peanuts a little more gently, which was difficult because of feeling angry inside. But having to be so still and gentle with the squirrels actually seemed to make me feel a little better. I wondered if feeding squirrels was a spy technique that Bill used for hypnotizing his victims.

The weird thing was that I started remembering that I *had* done this before. Not in this park. But I was in a red stroller, and someone was showing me how to throw the nuts gently so the squirrels would come and get them. I think the someone was Bill.

I kept dropping the peanuts closer and

closer to me, and the squirrels slowly got braver and braver, until they were so close I could see their little hands and their furry white tummies, so smooth and clean looking, and their tails curled up like feathers, and their hearts inside it all going pant pant pant. And then there were no peanuts left.

"Tell you what," said Bill, "I'm as hungry as those squirrels. How about we go and get something to eat?"

"Okay," I said. "Where shall we go?"

"I know a great little place just around the corner," he said mysteriously.

It was quite exciting. Maybe it would be a highly glamorous secret tennis club. Or a champagne and oyster bar. Or—

Well. No. It was the park café.

It was all pretty tacky-looking, with a swinging sign advertising ice cream, and parents sitting outside looking exhausted, while toddlers ran around screaming randomly like toddlers do.

BUT there was the most amazing smell coming from it. I stood there and sniffed. It smelled like hot vinegar, and golden-brown crispiness, and salt, and hot potatoness...

And I did remember eating chips with Bill in the café. Ages ago. It was fun. And afterward, we had ice cream.

And then he went away, and didn't come back for years.

"What d'you think, Bath?" He sounded all happy again. "Should we have some chips? They're not glamorous, but they taste fantastic."

Half of me wanted to say yes and half of me wanted to say no. But what I actually ended up saying was: "Why didn't you come and see me for *years*?"

It was meant to sound angry and indignant, but it came out as more of a wail. Bill's face went all funny, as if he was going to cry, and he said: "Let's go and sit down. I'll tell you over lunch."

We got a table near the window, where we could see the lake and the ducks gliding along and the geese peering distrustfully at everything.

Dear Diary, however horrible everything got afterward, I have to say that chips and beans and ice cream, though unhealthy and fattening, are Extraordinaciously Delicioso and I am going to get Natasha to make them every evening that Mother isn't around. Which means I can have them most nights, probably. Though I would rather have Mother.

But by the time it got to the ice cream, Bill was not looking happy at all. He hardly touched the sugar sprinkles. He looked a little sick. And then all of a sudden he said: "Bathsheba, you know, you come from a family of people with very active imaginations."

"Yes," I agreed. "I am creative and artistic, and so is Mother."

"That's one way of putting it," he said dryly. "Another is that we're always making things up. I remember my father. He was the biggest liar in town—" He stopped short, as if he had remembered something. "Anyway," he said, "I suppose you could say we're creative and artistic. Yes. That's the good side of it."

Ah hah! I thought. This huge feeling of relief just whooshed over me, like when you are paddling in the sea and a big wave comes out of nowhere and bowls you over, flump.

So THAT was why he hadn't come to see me!

It wasn't because he didn't love me!!

He was a Famous Artist, and had just been Wrapped Up in His Work!!!!

That was why he looked so shabby and boring! Everyone knows artists have no dress sense, especially famous ones!! Probably he would take me to live in his bohemian studio in Paris or New York!!! He would paint my portrait!!!!

He would—

"The bad side of it is that I have – in the past – been, well, a liar. A big liar. Dishonest."

I stared at him.

"See, the thing is –" he swallowed – "six years ago I was more creative and artistic than I should have been, at work. I was an accountant."

(An accountant!!!!! Yuck!!!!!!!!!!!!!!!!!!!!!!!!)

"I did something really, really stupid." He

did look very sick. I wondered if I should get him a bag. "I told some lies. A lot of lies. To do with money."

I had just put a spoonful of ice cream in my mouth, but suddenly I was listening too hard to swallow.

"Look, Bathsheba," he said, all in a rush. "I've been in prison for six years. For fraud. That's why I didn't come to see you before, I couldn't. I was locked up and I only got out the other day. I'm very, very sorry. I was an idiot. I'll never do it again. It took me away from you, for a start. Please, can you forgive me? I thought about you every day when I was inside. I sent you letters—"

I jumped up and ran to the bathroom and spat the ice cream all out in the sink as if it was toothpaste. Dear Diary, I nearly burst into tears right there. The only thing that stopped me was that there were lots of other girls in there too.

A CRIMINAL!!
A FRAUDSTER!!!
A CROOK!!

Oh! Oh! Oh! Oh! Oh! Oh! Oh!
Oh, dear Diary!!!!
My father is a thief!!

I am Bathsheba Clarice de Trop!!!!
I put thieves in prison!!!!
I should not be eating chips and beans with
one in the park!!!!
Oh!!!
I cannot have a criminal in the family.
It is Not Done!!!

I stormed back into the café and stormed
right out the door without even looking
at him.
"Bath! Wait!" He jumped up and rushed
after me.

(I think he stopped to pay the waitress. But as he is a CROOK, maybe not!!!!!!!!!!!!!!!!!!!!!!!!!!!)

He caught up with me just as I was going out of the park gates.

"Bathsheba! Please wait! I know it's a shock. I'm sorry. I'm really sorry!"

I tried to say something, but I just sort of bubbled with crying and snot.

"Please, Bath. I've served my sentence. I was stupid. I'm so sorry for everything. I'll make it up however I can."

"I want to go home," I sobbed.

"Okay. But calm down a little, first. Here, have a tissue." He handed me one.

I bubbled some more, into the tissue.

"Oh, dear," he said. "I love you, Bath. I'm so sorry."

Then he gave me a hug, which was ridiculous, because it was him who made me cry in the first place. But it still made me feel better, even though I didn't want it to. Only a little better, mind you. I still loathed him. He was a crook. A liar. Who deserted me.

"I NEVER WANT TO SEE YOU AGAIN!!!!!!" I told him, very loudly, so there was no mistake about it.

I started off down the road, and he hurried after me. When we got home, I did not say goodbye I just barged upstairs past Natasha when she opened the door, and shut myself in the vermilion closet, and *cried*, dear Diary, for about two hours.

o   o   o   o   o   o   o   o   o

Day Seven

I have not seen Bill again.
I don't care.
He is a CROOK.
I hate him.

o   o   o   o   o   o   o   o   o

Day Eight

Mother has been busy all week in meetings. When I tried to talk about Bill she just said, "Not *now*, dear," and took an aspirin.

Things are not much fun. No, dear Diary, they are pretty much all crud.

I wish Mother had given me Bill's letters instead of hiding them. At least I would have known where he was, and not have stupidly imagined he was an astronaut or something.

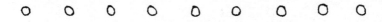

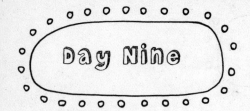

Day Nine

Natasha made chips last night, but it was not the same.

Mother is still really busy.

I wonder if fraud gets passed on, like brown eyes, for example.

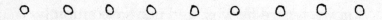

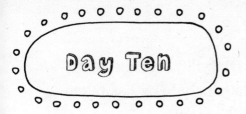
Day Ten

Dear Diary,

Oh wow, you will never, never guess what!!!

I am going to be a Movie Star!!!!!!!!!!!!!!!!!!!!!!!

Yes yes yes yes yes yes yes yes yes!!!!!

You know all the time Mother was busy?

She was in Negotiations with Twentieth Century Fox!

(They are a Very Huge Hollywood Film Production Company.)

Mother was on the phone for about three hours. I was sitting outside her study, wondering when she would come out, and I could hear her saying: "Yes...yes...yes...yes...no...yes...maybe..."

And when she came out of her study she was all pink with excitement and she

HUGGED me, dear Diary!!!!! And she said: "Marvelous news, Bathsheba! Fox has taken it. We're going to Hollywood!"

There is going to be a movie of the Bathsheba adventures!!!!!!!!!!!!!!!!!!!!!!!!!!

(Not all the adventures in the same movie, of course. That would be a very loooooooong movie. And slightly confusing!)

Mother is going to write a special script all about ME IN AMERICA, and then we're going to go there, and Twentieth Century Fox is going to film it!!!!

They must have heard about my Natural Acting Talent from Mother, and decided that a movie would be the perfect way to help me Break Into Hollywood. (Unlike my father, who is more likely to break into houses. Yuck. I don't want to think about that.)

I mean, it is completely perfect. Here is a movie all about ME, ME, ME and here am I – a fabulous young undiscovered actress. I will be able to play myself and of course I will do it *exquisatiously* because I *am* me, so I won't even have to try at all.

...Maybe I should rehearse being me, anyway, just in case...

Ooooooooo, dear Diary, it is going to be so *wonderabulously* amazing!!!!

I will have a trailer on set and people will shout "Take One!" at me!!!!

There will be clapperboards. Or clipperboards. Or something, anyway, those sort of very small blackboards like crocodiles.

I will finally find out what a Dolly Grip does.

I will get a Director's Chair and a Megaphone, so everyone can HEAR ME!!!

And of course I will get to kiss whoever

is playing Brad. Maybe Daniel Radcliffe is not busy this summer...

I will be a Star!!! (Even more than I am already!!!)

But it will not all be hard work, oh no, dear Diary, not if I can help it.

I will go shopping on Rodeo Drive, and put my hands in the concrete on Sunset Boulevard, and go to the beach and drink orange juice with HUGE sunglasses on!!!! (On me, not on the orange juice.)

And I will learn to rollerblade!!!!!

And Recline by the Pool!!!!!!

And Drawl!!!!!!!!

...Maybe I should get a little dog to put in my handbag?

Ooooooh, dear Diary, there is so much to think of and plan!

6:53 p.m. in the evening. (10:53 in the morning in Hollywood!)

Mother is going out to dinner with her Agent, to celebrate. I am having lasagna and chips with Natasha.

I sort of wish Bill were here so I could tell him about being a Movie Star. That would show him.

Huh, but he is probably off robbing a bank or something.

I will probably not see him again for years, if ever.

I don't care AT ALL. By then I will be a superstar actress and he will be sorry, oh yes.

I will not invite him to the premiere. Even if he begs and begs to come, which he won't, so I just won't think about it, that's all.

o o o o o o o O o

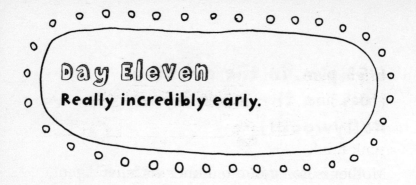

Day Eleven
Really incredibly early.

Wake up, dear Diary! Wake up!!

Today is a very special day!!!

It is the Hutchford's Book Signing and Bathsheba Bash.

(When you are a character in a best-selling book, book signings are like birthdays. Actually they are better than birthdays, because Mother usually forgets my birthday as it normally clashes with the Frankfurt Book Fair.)

I am so excited!!!!!!!!

There are going to be millions of fans there to see ME ME ME!!!!!!!!!!!!!!!!!!

We are going in a white limousine.

I am going to wear my ecru tutu,

bright blue
shoes, and
my hot
pink mink.

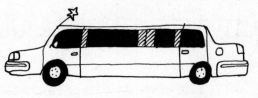

(Obviously a fake mink! Cruel is NOT
cool!!!)

Oooooooooo, it is going to be sooooo
magnificacious!!!!!

There is going to be a DJ and cake. (Lots
of cake.)

And it is all to celebrate the launch of
the Bathsheba Diary!!!!!

Yes, a diary just like you, dear Diary.

But far, far more glamorous!!!

It is gamboge with ecru ribbons and
mauve charms dangling off the bookmark.

It has glossy full-color pages so full of
quotes and illustrations from my books
that there is hardly any space to write
anything at all!!!!!!

It has also got:

☆ A pull-out list of my favorite foods. (Chips and beans is not on there, because that's a new one.)

☆ Press-out paper masks of Fifi and Aurelia and Brad. (Upgrade your friends by getting them to wear these super-glamorous disguises!!!)

☆ A pop-up pony. (Easier to take care of than a real one!!!!)

☆ Stickers. (Obviously!!!!! Stickers are great!!!!!!)

Dear Diary,

I have a little confession to make.

I WAS going to get a Bathsheba Diary myself, and chuck you in the garbage.

But I didn't.

Because, well, you are my best friend, and you have been there for me through Thick and Thin and Bill.

You listened to me and you did not laugh.

You did not say anything encouraging and sympathetic, but that was not your fault, as diaries cannot talk (however glamorous they are).

But you did LOOK about as encouraging and sympathetic as paper possibly can.

Anyway, I don't think one should throw a best friend in the garbage just because they are not as glamorous as they could be.

I would not like to be thrown in the garbage if I stopped being glamorous.

(And I sort of feel as if Aurelia and Fifi and Brad would probably have thrown me in the garbage if they had heard about Bill, because he is not a glamorous father at all.)

Anyway!!!

You are safe!!!!

AND, I am taking you in my bag to the Hutchford's Bathsheba Bash!!!!!

Lucky lucky lucky lucky lucky you!!!!!!

About lunchtime.

Dear Diary,

I am sitting in the staffroom at Hutchford's eating cake.

You would not believe how many rooms there are behind the actual bookstore. Squillions!!! And lots of long corridors with mysterious ancient people in them who I think are booksellers left over from before the war.

It is really spooky!!!

And there are Bathsheba books EVERYWHERE!!!!!!!

And Jo (the manager) is absolutely

fantastimazing. She said, "Wow, is this the heroine of all those fabulous books?" And she bought me a hot chocolate from the café (which I am drinking with the cake), and she gave me a special backpack with *Hutchford's* written on it, and a BADGE like the one the booksellers wear with a big blue H on it, so everyone knows I'm allowed to be in the staffroom.

We arrived here in the white limousine and there was a red carpet and there were loads of photographers and people waiting to get in. Obviously, I have been in loads of limousines before, but it was still exciting! Me and Mother bowed on the red carpet and everyone cheered and Mother hugged me lots, and there were flashbulbs going off all over the place. I practiced waving, for Hollywood.

And then we went inside, and there were PILES and PILES and PILES of Bathsheba books, dear Diary. I was overawed! And all the diaries were in HUGE, MOUNTAINOUS PYRAMIDS on top of tables.

I think you would have been a little scared by the diaries, dear Diary. They were very highly bred and glamorous, and there were a lot of them. I am glad you were safe in my bag!!!

The picture of Bathsheba on the front does not look quite like me. She looks older. And taller. And her teeth are whiter.

But nevermind. When I am in the movie playing myself, I will be on the covers of all the books and everyone will know exactly what I look like!!!

Actually, the book signing is going on right now, downstairs. I did go down. There was a huge busy line for Mother to sign the books. The DJ was playing music by Filthy Cake and The Heathers and The Dust Bunnies and lots of other cool bands, and it was really loud.

Lots of girls and boys were running around picking up copies of my books, but none of them came and talked to me. I suppose they were shy.

Anyway, everyone was very busy, either buying books or selling them or packing them in bags or reading them or dropping them on the floor and getting them kicked around, so I just sort of hung around behind Mother and tried to feel important. Mother kept signing books and smiling most beautifully as she handed them back.

"Thank you *so* much," she kept saying. "*So* kind. Have you bought a diary yet?"

In the end I wandered off awhile and read some other books in a corner by myself. I read the Dramarama journals. Dramarama is a special international summer camp for children from all over the world who want to be actors and movie stars. They make TV shows about it, and write books about it too, with all kinds of fabulous acting tips in them, like how to do stunts safely and staying in character even when everyone is staring at you horribly. I would so love to go on a Dramarama camp, but you have to be extraordinarily good at acting, and your teacher has to recommend you.

Then all of a sudden Mother was standing there, looking pink and excited, next to two security guards and a really tall, slim, gorgeous girl. The girl had long, wavy, almost white-blonde hair all the way down her back, and a really deep tan, and HUGE sunglasses, just like I'm going to have when I'm a Movie Star. She was wearing extremely cool jeans, which were definitely Gucci, and loads of funky jewelry *and* makeup *and* high-heeled boots. She looked about nineteen.

"Hey, wow, it is like, sooooo cool to be here," she was saying. "This, like, sooooo rocks."

"Bathsheba!" Mother looked really excited.

"I want you to meet Avocado Dieppe."

(Avocado????????????)

"She's an up-and-coming actress. She's already been in a really successful TV series in America. And she's going to be in the movie! Why don't you two girls bond? You must have so much in common! I must go and finish the signing now, Avocado dear."

I was a little overawed, dear Diary. (Plus, I wasn't at all sure I'd heard her name right.) I wondered who she would play in the movie. Maybe one of the bad guys.

"Hi," I said nervously.

"*Hi!!!!!!*" she said.

Her "Hi" was definitely better than mine. Her teeth were whiter, for a start. They sort of glowed.

"Gee," said Avocado (??). "What a quaint little bookstore!"

Dear Diary, I am not sure what quaint means, but Hutchford's is not little.

"Everything is so teeny-weeny here," said Avocado. "Like your limo! It's soooo tiny!"

"It's not!!"

"Sure it is!" She grinned at me with her luminous teeth. "I have a huge limo," she told me. "It's as big as this store! Actually, I've got, like, six limos!"

I was going to say I didn't believe her, but she didn't give me a chance.

"I have three ponies," she told me. "I sure miss them! But they wouldn't fit in my private jet!"

"I'm head of my school," I said.

"Oh, gee, I go to such a darling, amazing school in Hollywood! It's called a boarding school but it's really more like a summer camp for actresses and models! We have our own stables and private flying school and beauty salon and theater! It's called St. Agnes'. St. Agnes' is just soooooo cool! It's full of people just like me!"

Dear Diary, she just did not shut up at all after that!!!!!

"I've got this" and "I've got that" and so on until I was SO BORED I WAS PRACTICALLY DEAD.

Dear Diary, I do not know about you, but I think it is just plain RUDE when people SHOW OFF like that.

Who cares about her three ponies?

Who cares about her personal hairdresser??

Who cares about her yacht???

NOT ME.

I think Avocado (or whatever her name is... Avocado?? Is that possible???) needs a lesson in GOOD MANNERS.

And considering other people's feelings!!!

She is NOT Princesscular!!!!

I was just about to say so (if I could have got a word in edgeways) when she SCREAMED. *Maybe it's the Peruvians at last!* I thought.

But no.

"Oh my gosh! There are just my most best friends in, like, the universe! Arabella and Kiki from St. Agnes'!"

I looked around and saw two girls, who were almost as thin and gorgeous as Avocado, running over toward us. They had perfect nails and perfect jeans just like Avocado's, and they were wearing high heels with strappy glittery pieces, and they had really expensive bags made out of what looked like crocodile skin, only there is no such thing as a hot pink crocodile. One of them had really long, straight, rich chestnut hair which she kept flicking around, and the other one had curly red hair and glasses, but extremely cool glasses (the sort you would wear with no lenses in just to look trendy).

"Avocado! *Hi!!!!*"

"Kiki! Arabella! Mwah! Mwah!"

I got sort of squashed in the middle, as they were much taller than me (even without the heels), so I struggled out before I suffocated.

"Hi!" I said, but they completely ignored me, and just talked over my head to Avocado. Arabella flicked her hair back and forth madly so I kept having to duck.

"Did Jake call?"

"Noooo! But guess what? I've got a date with Rufus next Friday!!"

"Cooool!! Do you like my new bag?? It's Kenzo!!"

"Oh, yeah! Wow! I just *love* Kenzo!"

"Me too!"

"I've got a big dollhouse," I said, but not very loudly.

Anyway, dear Diary, it made absolutely no difference at all. I could probably have shouted at the top of my voice, "My father is a CROOK!" and they would still just have completely and totally ignored me.

SO RUDE.

(And mean!!!)

So I came back upstairs to the staffroom instead.

The window is open and I can hear lots of girls and boys and their mothers and fathers talking and laughing as they line up to be let in. They do not seem to mind that it is raining.

...Huh, dear Diary, when I wrote *fathers* just then, I suddenly thought, *Bill is my father*.

I mean, I know he's my father. But does that mean he's like, my dad???

I don't think he is quite a dad. To be a dad, you have to do stuff like complain about phone bills and hog the TV and make one do the dishes and give one rides to ballet class. You need to be there for that – it takes a lot of effort. And Bill was not there for years and years. He is not even here right now.

...I wonder what he is doing instead?

He said he was going to be here. He said he would buy a ticket.

He probably can't be bothered, or has forgotten about me already.

Not that I care.

Later.

After the book signing it started to rain even harder, and although I tried to concentrate on being a Star in Hollywood, it was hard to imagine lounging by the pool when small tourists were being washed away by the floods in Regent Street. When I got home, I Mooched upstairs and Mooched around my room awhile. (Mooching is a miserable sort of walk, it is like a whole body sort of shrug; your shoulders go up and down and your arms go sort of floppy and you look as if you have sagged in the middle and are about to DIE because you are SO BORED.)

Then I lay on my back on the bed with my legs up the wall and pretended that gravity had stopped working and I was on the ceiling...

Then I went under my bed and discovered things, like a sock and half a cookie and a small pink plastic flamingo...

There was really nothing to do, and HOURS till dinner time.

I started thinking: *If I am going to play myself in the movie, then maybe I should know more about myself. Like, maybe, about Bill.*

It is called Motivation, my mother explained it once. Like if someone owns thirteen cats, then it is probably because they could not have any children. Or because they have a lot of mice. Or because they just like cats.

I like cats.

Anyway.

It is not because I care about Bill or anything.

I went downstairs and knocked on the door of Mother's study.

"...Mother?" I put my head around the door.

"Yes, Bathsheba?" She frowned. "Is that strawberry jam on your fingers?"

"No, vermilion nail polish."

"Well, make sure you don't get it on anything."

I collected my thoughts. Mother always does this, I try to ask her something, and then it turns out I have Nutella on my top or something and next thing I know I have completely forgotten what I meant to say.

"Have you – did you—" I swallowed. "You know Bill sent me letters?"

She went very still. "Oh yes."

"Well...I mean, did you – er – keep them?"

There was a pause.

"Yes," she said, with a sigh. "Why?" Instead of waiting for me to reply, she said, "I suppose you want to read them? To be honest, I have been regretting keeping them from you. It may have been a mistake. I meant it for the best."

"I don't really mind," I said. "I mean, I was just wondering."

But she was already looking through her desk, and then she held out a bunch of letters to me. They were written in blobby blue ballpoint on very ugly notepaper with *H.M.P. Podcaster* stamped on it.

It was weird, holding them, and thinking that Bill wrote them when he was Locked Up. I wondered what it was like being in prison. I wondered if they fed you enough or only passed strips of stuff through the bars. I wondered if you had to wear miserable gray pajamas all day, and possibly have your legs tied together with chains.

It must have been horrible.

Poor Bill.

"Try not to get any nail polish on them," said Mother, but only sort of automatically. I could tell her thoughts were Elsewhere.

Well, dear Diary.

It was very, very weird reading Bill's letters.

It was like a Voice out of the Mists of the Past.

The thing is that actually he sounds quite cheerful in them at first. He is laughing about the food and the horrible prison wardens and the yucky toilets. And then he writes: *I miss you, Bath. I'm so sorry this happened. I hope one day you'll forgive me.* And suddenly you realize that he's not cheerful at all. He feels like crud, and he's just pretending.

Maybe we are similar after all.

I have a funny feeling in my tummy, like I don't know whether I'm sad or angry or sorry for him or what.

Maybe it is a little of everything.

Maybe I might like to talk to him again. One day.

o   o   o   o   o   o   o   o   o

Dear Diary,
My life is RUINED.

I have only you now.

No one will ever be my friend, and it is all horrible Keisha's fault and horrible Avocado's fault.

I have had the most horrible press conference ever.

It was totally, totally humiliating!

I almost didn't go and I wish I hadn't now. I was just coming downstairs and I saw Mother was in her best white suit with a little white hat, just about to go out of the door. There was a taxi outside with the engine running.

"Bathsheba, I'm off to the press conference for the movie," she said, grabbing her coat and hurrying down the steps.

"Me too!" I bounced down the steps with her and scrambled into the taxi.

"You want to come? Oh." She climbed in next to me, looking a little confused. "It will be really boring, you know," she said. "And it might go on for a long time, we've invited the local press and school newspapers."

"It won't be boring if I'm there," I told her.

Thank heavens, I thought, *even though my family life is a Tragedy, my Career is Blossoming.*

Oh, dear Diary, little did I know!!!!

The press conference started off okay. There was me and Mother and Avocado. (I didn't know why she bothered coming, but I thought maybe she had nothing else to do – HAH!!!) Mother answered nice questions like, "Where do you get your inspiration?" ("From my darling daughter, Bathsheba.") and "How long does it take to write a book?" ("Oh, not long. Just a couple of days.") and "Why do you only wear white?" ("White is such a *spiritual* color.")

Then the first awful thing happened.

When Mother's agent said, "Anymore questions for Mrs. de Trop?" someone stood up and said, "No, but I've got a question for Bathsheba."

It was her!

A Little Princess!!

Natasha's goddaughter!!!

The one I'd thought had a friendly face. (HAH!!!)

Only not wearing a silk dress now, of course. Her curly black hair was done in a grown-up sort of way, and she had a jacket like reporters wear on television, all shoulder pads and camouflage print. She looked very cool, but still nice (HAH again!)

"Keisha Freeman, Clotborough School Junior Reporter of the Year, *Clotborough School Gazette*. Bathsheba, good morning," she said, sounding completely confident and as if she did press conferences all the time.

"Good morning," I said a little squeakily.

(Clotborough School Junior Reporter of the Year?)

"Bathsheba, how does it feel to be the daughter of a best-selling novelist?"

"Fantastic!!" I said. "My life is fabulous!!!"

She raised an eyebrow, like lawyers do.

"But don't you ever find yourself getting a little, well, jealous of the other Bathsheba and her amazing life? I mean, everything's so perfect for her, isn't it?"

"But I *am* Bathsheba," I said. "There isn't another one."

Everyone laughed. I have no idea why. Suddenly it felt as if the room was a little too hot and a lot too full. I could feel myself going red.

"Oh yes, of course you've got the same name. But the Bathsheba in the books is totally different from you," she said, SMILING!!! "You've never saved the world, for example."

"I have!!! Thirteen times!!!!! Once from giant bees, twice from terrorists, once from smugglers, once from *other* smugglers that time the president was kidnapped—" I stopped because *everyone* was laughing.

"But not really," said horrible, HORRIBLE Keisha. "It's made up. Everyone knows that. I mean, the president's never been kidnapped at all, so how could you have saved him?"

I opened my mouth and shut it again. I tried to will Mother to tell Keisha to shut up. But when I looked over at her she was not even listening, she was making notes on a piece of paper and whispering to *slimy* Avocado.

"I just think," said Keisha, "that my readers would be very interested to hear it from your point of view – how it feels to sort of NOT be Bathsheba."

There was a most horrible silence. It is bad enough thinking you are going to cry, but thinking it while sitting in front of about a million people, who are all STARING at you, is much, much worse.

Keisha looked slightly embarrassed, as if she couldn't understand why I wasn't answering.

"Do you ever wish you went to a school like St. Barnaby's?" she asked me.

I forced myself to say something.

"I do go to St. Barnaby's. I am head of everything there, and I have best friends there, Fifi and Aurelia—"

"Really?" She looked puzzled. "But a very good source –" (HORRIBLE NATASHA!!!!!!!) – "says you have been homeschooled by tutors all your life and have never been to school at all. Don't you find it hard to make friends?"

"I think we need to stop there," interrupted Mother's agent hastily, who appeared to be the ONLY one who had noticed how I was feeling. "Mrs. de Trop, would you like to...?"

Oh, dear Diary, I bet you thought it couldn't get any worse.

Well, HA.

Ha ha ha ha ha ha ha ha ha ha ha.

Because Mother coughed into her microphone, and said: "Yes, I have an extremely exciting announcement to make!"

I started feeling a little better.

"The movie will star a very special young actress."

I got ready to bow. *Ha*, I thought. *Ha, stupid horrible Junior Reporter Keisha of the Year, I bet you aren't a Hollywood Movie Star. Ha!*

"So young, yet so talented – a real face of the future!"

Blush blush blush blush blush blush blush!!!
"We are delighted to announce that
Bathsheba Clarice de Trop will be played by
Avocado Dieppe!"

I do not really remember what happened
after that, but dear Diary, I have locked myself
in the bathroom and I am never coming out.

Later. ♡ ☆

FINE!!
OKAY!!!
So it's not true.

I don't have amazing best friends. I don't
have any friends at all, actually.

And I don't go to previews or the opera or
horse races. Because I have no friends to go
with.

I don't go to a select boarding school. I just

have Miss Kipper, who comes over to teach me, and smells of fish.

And I don't have a boyfriend. And I've never saved the world.

And I'm not head of any drama club and I'm not a champion showjumper. (But I do have two ponies, even though I never see them as Mother is always too busy to take me to the stables.)

And FINE, Miss SMUG, HORRIBLE Keisha, I am NOT Junior Reporter of anything!

I don't care, I don't care, I don't care, well yes actually I do care, but I am not telling Miss snottyhorriblemeanyucky Girl Reporter that.

Who on earth would ever want to know me if they knew how totally, utterly BORING my life is?????

Nobody wants to be friends with an unglamorous, lonely, boring LOSER.

No, they want to be friends with the

Bathsheba who saves the world, and always gets everything right, and has good hair.

Oh oh oh oh oh oh oh oh.

I am just a total, total loser.

I have never saved the president and I have never been to a beach party.

I do not have a boyfriend and at this rate I probably never will.

I cannot ice skate.

And no one will ever be my friend because I am just TOO BORING.

And now some horrible person is knocking at the door.

Oh, hang on, dear Diary. I think it's Mother. She must have followed me when I ran off crying.

Later still. ♡ ◎

I wouldn't let Mother in – she sounded really
angry.

"What on earth is going on?" she said.
"Why did you storm out in front of all those
reporters?"

"You gave that horrible girl my part!" I told
her. "No one could ever play Bathsheba as
well as me! Why didn't you tell me you were
giving it to her instead of making me look
totally stupid?"

"What? But, Bathsheba, I had no idea you
wanted to be in the movie!"

"Duh! What is the point of a movie about
Bathsheba if it doesn't star Bathsheba?? And
of course I want to be in a movie. I'm going
to be a Movie Star when I grow up! It's my
Doom!"

There was a little pause, and then Mother
said, "I think you mean it's your destiny. And

I'm sorry you're upset, but I didn't even know you wanted to be a movie star."

"Well, that's just because you're always so busy you never have time to find out anything about me, ever, at all!!!" I shouted.

The next thing I heard was Mother walking away from the door. *Oh no,* I thought. *Now she's* really *angry.* I opened the door a crack and peered out. Mother was standing next to a potted plant, talking on her cell phone. She listened for a second, rubbing her forehead as if she had a headache, and then she said, "She's locked herself in the bathroom and she won't come out. I'm at my wits' end. Can you do something? Get her out somehow?"

I don't know who she was talking to. Maybe the fire department? Are they going to come and knock down the door with a bulldozer? I closed the door very quickly.

I've decided I won't come out even if bricks

start tumbling down around my head. I wonder if I could become famous as the only Movie Star in the world who lives in a bathroom in a bookstore. They could make movies of me through the keyhole, and feed me on anything that fit under the door, like very thin ham.

Oh wait a minute. Now someone ELSE is outside. And they're shouting my name.

Well, they will just have to pee elsewhere. I don't care.

Hang on, dear Diary.
It's Bill!!

Nearly dinner time.

Dear Diary,
You'll never guess where I am.

In the café at the Natural History Museum!

It is actually very cool here. It's like a palace, and you walk in under a huge arch like a stone rainbow. Inside there is the biggest staircase I've ever seen in all my life, and statues. There are amazing carved stone walls with monkeys and birds peering out of them. And there are gorgeous paintings of flowers way, way up on the ceilings – which are Enormously High.

And the dinosaur skeleton really is the size of a bus!

I would be quite enjoying myself if my life were not ruined.

Speaking of buses, I did not know sitting at the front of the top deck of a bus could be so exciting. It is better than being in a limousine because you can look down on all the people and watch them doing everything, especially as the bus goes so slowly since it is always stuck in traffic. It is like being at the movies.

Anyway, dear Diary, I expect you want to

know what I am doing here.

Well, when I realized it was Bill at the door, obviously I shouted "Go away!!!" really loudly. And "I hate you!!!!"

"But, Bath, there's someone out here who wants to use the bathroom."

I opened the door a crack.

"No there isn't!"

Bill put his foot in the door before I could close it.

"Come on, pet. Don't feel so bad about it. I hear Hollywood is boring this time of year, anyway. Why not come and have lunch with me instead? We could go to the Natural History Museum café, and see the dino skeleton at the same time!"

"Oh yeah, right, just like that? Huh! Where were you? You just abandoned me!"

"Well, you said you never wanted to see me again, so I thought I'd better leave you alone awhile. But I didn't forget about you. I've been checking in with your mother on the phone, to make sure you were okay. And to see when I could visit again."

"Huh," I said. Oh.

"But then your mother called me and explained what happened at the press conference... Come on, Bath. You can't stay in there forever. What are you going to eat, toilet paper?"

I tried not to smile, but it was a little difficult: I could just imagine me with a mouthful of toilet paper, like a donkey eating straw.

"What about Mother?" I said.

"I asked her and she said, 'If you can get her out of that bathroom you can take her to China for all I care.'"

(I wish I could go to China. There are pandas there. They might be my friends.)

Anyway, at last I came out of the bathroom, and we went on the bus to the Natural History Museum.

After we had been to see all the cool things, like the Tyrannosaurus Rex (which really moves as if he's going to eat you!), and the Blue Whale hanging from the ceiling (even bigger than the dinosaur skeleton!), and the 1,300-year-old tree (which was alive when *A Little Princess* was being written!) and been in the Earthquake Machine (cool but scary!), we finally went to get chips at the café.

I got three different kinds of sauce, and I was mopping them up sadly with my chips, when Bill said: "You know your mother's books aren't real, don't you, Bath?"

I pushed a chip into my mouth and didn't say anything.

"Bath? Come on. I know you're not silly. You know they're not real, don't you?"

I chewed and swallowed.

"Yes," I muttered.

"Good."

After a while, he said: "You know, when I

was at school I used to tell all the other boys that I was a car thief."

I stared at him.

"Were you?"

He laughed.

"No way! I just thought no one would be interested in me if I didn't make up an exciting life for myself. I thought I was a genuine wimp, specially compared to my old man, but maybe if I told people I was a car thief they'd think I was cool and exciting, and they'd want to be my friends."

"And did they?"

"Some people did. But they turned out to be bad friends. I wished I'd never met them in the end."

He stole a chip while I was staring at him. Huh!!!

"Then, ages later, I met your mother. Well, she was a cut above me. She was used to a certain kind of 'lifestyle' and it cost a lot. I'm not blaming her – I was the one who did the lying and the stealing. No one's fault except my own. But I was a little out of my league with her. I thought she'd never like me unless I had loads of money and a really cool, glamorous lifestyle. So that's when I started stealing from work. Just a little at first. And then more...and more...and more. I was completely stupid, Bath. You know, I was almost glad when I got caught. It meant at least I could finally stop pretending."

He looked at me really seriously.

"I can't do much to make it up to the people whose money I stole, but I can try and make it up to you. I can try by being a good dad for you, the best dad I can possibly be. I don't want a glamorous life anymore. I don't care what anyone thinks of me. I just care that you think I'm a great dad."

I was slightly worried I was going to cry again, or do something embarrassing like hug him, so I carefully dropped my fork so I could go under the table and calm down.

All the fashion gurus say you can tell everything about a person from what kind of shoes they wear. Bill's shoes were old white tennis shoes, muddy and a little smelly, but they had a friendly, sort of cheerful look about them. I wondered if I should buy him some new shoes with my allowance when I went to America. (Because I suppose I will still have to go to America with Mother. I mean, I don't think she would let me stay in the house by myself for months and months.) Oddly enough, the thought of going to America did not make me as excited as it had just the other day. It is not so much fun Reclining and Drawling if one is not a Star but a Loser whose life is completely ruined. And I should think that they only allow Stars to carry little dogs in their handbags, at any rate I have never seen a real person do it, only celebrities.

And then I thought: *America is quite a long way from Bill.*

I suddenly felt really guilty and awful, because I knew he had been hoping to eat chips and beans with me and so on, and now it wasn't going to happen, because I was going away.

I surfaced, feeling low and small.

"Bill," I said, "you know about the movie that's going to be made?"

"I bet you would have done a much better job than that silly Avocado," he said, cheerfully stealing another chip. "Avocado! Huh! What kind of a name is that, anyway?"

"Um," I said. "It's just – have you ever thought of going to America?"

He laughed.

"I can't afford a vacation, chick. I was thinking of moving closer to you and your mother. Then I could see you more easily. Most of my money will be going toward rent."

"Well, but, if you want to see me easily, you might have to move to America," I said unhappily.

He dropped the chip he was holding.

"Oh, no. You're going over? Both of you? You have to?"

I nodded.

I felt terrible, dear Diary, especially when, after fumbling miserably for the dropped chip awhile, he said, in a fake happy voice that was obviously just trying to make me feel better: "Well, I'm really happy for you. How exciting!" But he couldn't keep it up. "Oh, Bath, I'll really miss you."

"I don't suppose you want to go out with Mother again?" I said, hopefully. "Then you could come too."

I didn't actually think it was going to work, I was just Clutching at Straws. Bill smiled, but in such a sad way that I knew there was absolutely no hope of that ever. It was probably a good thing as he would be certain to put his feet on the furniture at some point, and then they would just have to split up all over again.

Bill sort of hauled his face into a smile.

"Never mind, chick," he said. "Maybe we could meet up before you go, like twice a week, and go for chips or see a movie or something. What do you think? Make the most of the time?"

I hesitated. Part of me was thinking: *That would be fun*. Part of me was thinking, *Mmm, chips*. But another – quite a big – part of me was thinking:

What if I see him for a few weeks and we have a lot of fun?

What if I really enjoy it?

What if it is like having a real dad? What if he takes me to book signings and to the park and claps when I act in *A Little Princess*?

And then what if he stops coming?

Forever?

I swallowed.

Bill's face fell.

"I know you probably have other things to do," he said. "I suppose twice a week seems like a lot to you." He stared at his chips. "It doesn't to me, though. I've really missed you."

Oh, dear Diary, help!!!!!

o o o o o o o o o

Day Thirteen

Dear Diary,
I am so miserable.

I keep thinking about Bill. I do not know what the right thing to do is.

I do not want to start liking him and then have him rob a bank or something and go away again for years.

I know he said he would never do it again, but can I trust him?

I do not want to start liking him and then have to go to America and when I come back find out that he has forgotten all about me.

I tried to do some acting, but I do not have the heart. Keisha has spoiled it all by making me look like a total idiot in front of EVERYBODY.

My room is completely boring, and there is

nothing to do, and I have nothing to wear.

What can I do to make myself feel better?

I tried smiling in the mirror, but frankly it was a loss, because my teeth do not glow like Avocado's. (Honestly, they sort of floated. It was like Casper the Friendly Ghost or something.)

I know!

Where is my copy of *A Little Princess* – oh yes, here it is under the bed...

I knew I would find something in here that would help. Listen to this, dear Diary!

When things are horrible – just horrible – I think as hard as ever I can of being a princess. I say to myself, "I am a princess, and I am a fairy one, and because I am a fairy nothing can hurt me or make me uncomfortable."

I shall think as hard as I can of being Princesscular!

Hmm. How shall I be a princess?

Well, princesses are Gracious and Kind. And they walk with dignity, they do not Mooch or Mope, which is what I am doing at the moment. They have a different walk. They Swan.

I shall Swan.

This is like walking with a very straight back and your nose in the air, with your toes dragging along the ground like a train. (I don't mean an actual train. It's a piece of cloth that drags around after your dress, like a mermaid tail.)

I should have a train as well!!!

I think the curtains will do, if I fix them up with tape.

Later (after having Swanned).

Well, things are still horrible, only more so.

I Swanned downstairs. I Swanned past the kitchen.

Natasha came out. Huh! I am ignoring her – TRAITOR!!!!!

"Bath," she called, "hang on a minute. I want to explain about yesterday."

"It's all right, Natasha," I said Graciously and Kindly. "I forgive you. Your own guilty conscience will be punishment enough."

She laughed.

"Oh, Bath. Don't be like that. I just wanted to say that Keisha didn't mean to upset you."

"Yeah, RIGHT," I said, coming UnSwanned for a minute. Thankfully I remembered to be a little Princesscular. "I pity Keisha, I do not hate her," I told Natasha, and Swanned off.

Unfortunately one of the things about

Swanning is that you can't really see where you're going, which is all right if you are a princess and have ladies-in-waiting to tell you to look out for cliffs and things, but I do not have ladies-in-waiting. I Swanned straight into the bathroom door and got quite a bad bump. Huh, ouch.

"Why are you walking like that anyway?" said Natasha as she put ice on my bump.

"Because I am a princess," I said irritably, "and they Swan."

"Where did you read that, *Swann's Way?*" she said, and started laughing so hard she dropped the ice. I HATE it when people laugh at you like that, it is not FAIR. I stormed off upstairs.

I am glad I have you, dear Diary, I would be really, really miserable otherwise.

o   o   o   o   o   o   o   o   o

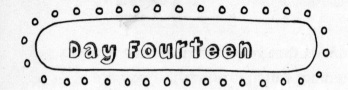

Dear Diary,

I just had a conversation with Mother.

She called me into her office, and said "Bathsheba, are you all right? Don't lean on the desk, it's just been polished."

I nodded.

She frowned at me.

"Natasha said you're not feeling very happy?"

I shrugged.

"I realize things have been a little awkward recently. I want you to know that I wasn't expecting him to turn up out of the blue. I would have said something, if I'd known he was coming... I'm glad you are being so sensible about it all. I do feel he deserves a chance, after all."

It took me a minute to realize that she was talking about Bill.

Mother ran her hand through her hair so it stuck out sideways just like mine does. "I'm sorry," she said. "I should probably have noticed you were having a hard time. It's been so complicated – with your father – and then the movie... I really do – er – do my best, you know. I know I'm busy a lot, but it's all to promote the Bathsheba brand. Do you understand?"

I nodded. She looked grateful.

"I mean – the Bathsheba brand is your inheritance. We want it to be perfect, don't we? I sell these books for *you*, you know – so you can afford everything you want. And we must have a real actress for the movie. It's very important. You do understand, don't you, why it can't be you in the starring role?"

I nodded.

"So what's the matter?"

I swallowed.

"It's just – I don't know who to *be*."

Mother blinked. I could tell she didn't get it. I didn't really get it myself, to be honest. I just knew it was true.

"Be, dear? I thought you wanted to be a movie star?"

"I do!"

"Well, perhaps we can arrange something!" She got all busy and pleased, the way she does when she's got something to organize, and started making notes with a silver pencil in a little white suede notebook. "Yes, good heavens, we are going to Hollywood, acting capital of the world, after all! I'm sure I can arrange something. You could have a small part in the movie, why not?" She smiled at me happily. "You feel better now, don't you?"

Dear Diary, I nodded, because honestly, what else was there to do?

Bath time. ♡ ☆

I am writing this in the jaccuzzi, dear Diary.
I will try not to drop you.

This next part is SECRET. You must never
tell anyone, because they would all laugh.

I don't want to be a brand. I want to be me.
But I don't know how to be.

Because I'm not a princess, and I'm not
Bathsheba. I don't know who I am at all.

That is why I feel so unhappy. It is not
America, or Keisha, at all, really.

It is me.

On the other hand, Mother has called Bill,
and he is coming over on Friday to take me
for chips in the park.

I wish I knew how I felt about that.

But since I do not even know how to be me,
I have obviously less than no hope of knowing
how to feel about anything, ever, at all.

o   o   o   o   o   o   o   o   o

Day Fifteen

Dear Diary,

Crud, crud and double crud!!!

I cannot believe we bumped into her!!!!

What total utter cruddy luck!!!!!

I was just sitting in the park café with Bill, when I heard this voice that sounded familiar.

"There she is! By the window!"

And there, dear Diary, on the other side of the café, was the smiley, round woman who was sitting next to me at the play (who turned out to be Keisha's mother, Bev).

And with her was Keisha!!! Wearing rollerblades, and very muddy around the knees.

They were staring right at us!!!

Bev poked Keisha in the ribs.

"Off you go! Right now!"

"Oh no!" I turned to Bill. "It's that horrible girl from the press conference! She's probably going to shout at me and tell me I'm a liar and—"

"It's okay, Bath. Just stay calm and see what she wants."

Keisha rolled over to us. (It was quite impressive how she balanced so well.) As she came closer I could see she looked really worried and upset.

Guess what she said to me?

"Sorry."

!!!

"I just thought it would be a good article – how the real Bathsheba wasn't like the Bathsheba in the books – I didn't mean to upset you!"

I didn't really know what to say. I didn't know if I should believe her or not. Part of

me was thinking *YEAH, RIGHT*, and part
of me was thinking, *Oh*.

"She really is sorry," said Bev,
coming up behind her, and speaking to Bill.
She was VERY round and VERY smiley. "I
hope we're not disturbing you. But I thought
Keisha should apologize for upsetting you."

"I'm really sorry," said Keisha. "I didn't
know you thought it was *real*."

I felt completely stupid. I turned red and
Glowered at her.

"OBVIOUSLY it's not real! I didn't think
it was AT ALL!"

"Okay, Bath, that's enough," said Bill
hurriedly. He smiled at Keisha and Bev
as if they were friends or something. "Why
don't you sit down? Pull up a chair?"

"Well, I don't mind if we do," said Keisha's
round, smiley, totally unhelpful mother.

Bill frowned at me and made eyebrow
motions at my plate of chips.

CRUD!!!!!!!! I thought.

"Do you want a chip?" I mumbled to Keisha.

"Cool," said Keisha. "Thanks!"

I was glad to see that at least she had the manners to take a polite-sized chip (not the biggest one on the plate, and not one of the little crispy ones either, as people often like those the best).

I sat scowling while Bill and Bev talked about stupid stuff like house prices. Keisha reached out for another chip.

"I said 'a' chip, not lots!" I snarled.

"Oh." She looked a little upset and embarrassed. Hah, serves her right, now she knows what it feels like!

"Look, I honestly am sorry," she said under her breath. "I don't know why you're so angry anyway, if you knew it wasn't real. I thought you'd *want* to tell your side of it."

"I'm not angry," I said angrily. Then I added, because I couldn't help being curious, "Junior

Reporter of the Year? What's that about, huh?"

"It's just something I do at school. We've got a newspaper, and I'm editor. And there was this competition, and I won."

"Yes, well, you can stop showing off about it now!"

"I wasn't showing off – you asked!"

"Huh!"

We didn't say anything for a while. I kept thinking about her in the play, and I started feeling a little less angry and a little more curious about her. I wouldn't have said anything, obviously, but Bill suddenly leaned over and said: "Why don't you visit Bath sometime, Keisha? I bet she would love to have a friend come over. She likes acting too, don't you, Bath?"

I made horrified eyebrow motions at Bill, but he ignored me completely!

"That would be lovely, wouldn't it, Keish?"

said Bev, as if she'd been promised a trip to Disneyland or something.

"Oh," said Keisha, doubtfully, "cool."

We glanced at each other suspiciously, and I could tell we were thinking the exact same thing: *Parents, huh!*

"In fact," said Bill, "how about tomorrow? You two girls can hang out, and Keisha, your mother can take me to see some of those houses we've just been talking about."

"Um," said Keisha.

"WELL, Bathsheba?" said Bill, in a father sort of voice. "Wouldn't that be nice?"

"Yeah," I muttered. And, since my crook of a father obviously wanted me to LIE, I said, "I can't wait."

Keisha may be super-junior-mega-reporter-actress-star girl, but she obviously does not understand sarcasm, because she smiled, and said, "Okay! I'd really like that too!"

After they had FINALLY gone, I said to Bill, "I can't believe you did that! Are you trying to totally ruin my life even more than it is already?"

"No," he said. "I just think you ought to make some friends, that's all."

"Huh, with snotty Keisha? No way!!!"

"She seems like a lovely girl. Just give her a chance. Go on – for me." He did big puppy eyes. "You'll be going off to America soon, and I want to know that you've made some friends, that you're not spending all your time in your own imagination."

Ugh, yuck. I am being blackmailed.

I hoped Mother would say no to having Keisha visit, but she said, "Why yes, dear, have a friend come over, of course!"

Huh!

Tomorrow is going to be completely awful.

I suppose I will just have to live through it,

as I have lived through so many other disappointments and setbacks in my short but tragic life.

Sigh, dear Diary, sigh, sigh, sigh.

o   o   o   o   o   o   o   o   o

Day Sixteen

Dear Diary,
Wow, gosh, well, you'll never guess what!

Keisha is actually really nice!!!

I have snuck off and am pretending to be using the bathroom. Keisha is still trying on my clothes. She was so impressed with my room! She said, "Wow, you have seven closets! That's so amazing! You're so so lucky!" And she has all kinds of fabulous ideas about what to do with my clothes, like I never thought of putting the hot pink boots with the mauve belt and the bright blue dress, but she did, and it looks fantastabulous.

And she's made my hair into braids with pieces of colored ribbons and tied them with beads! It looks soooo cool!

Oh, dear Diary, I am so nervous though, because this is the only chance I have to make completely certain that she wants to be my friend!!! And how am I going to do that when she knows I am actually completely boring, and have never saved the world and have no boyfriend or anything?? I have to impress her!!!

I bet you are wondering how come I suddenly like her. Well, to be honest I am wondering that myself, too.

It didn't start off so well. When the doorbell rang Mother opened the door, and there was Keisha, looking very neat and polite, and with no rollerblades (so shorter) and no mud, and instead a white dress that I bet her mother made her wear. Natasha took Keisha's coat, which was a little weird for everyone, because of Natasha being Keisha's godmother and our housekeeper.

Keisha was really quiet and she stared at

everything as if she was in a palace or something. I think she would have just turned around and run out if she could, and actually, I really wanted her to. But I felt a little smug, because even if I am not interesting and exciting and glamorous, I do at least have a really amazing house with three living rooms.

But princesses are not supposed to feel like that (although I bet they do) so instead, I Swanned over and shook her hand graciously, and said "How do you doooo?" in my fanciest voice.

Mother took us into the biggest living room, and Natasha brought us orange juice. Keisha sat on the edge of her chair and hung on to her glass like if she let go she would fall through the floor or something. I sipped my juice in a Princesscular fashion and tried to remember not to put my feet on the furniture.

"Where do you live, Keisha?" asked Mother.

"Clotborough Estates," said Keisha.

Mother nearly spilled her orange juice.

"Good heavens! I mean – isn't it awfully dangerous?"

"Oh no. Only if you go down the south side," said Keisha.

"I've heard – well, of course, these things get exaggerated…"

Mother got all flustered after that, and sent us upstairs.

"Your home is so beautiful!" said Keisha as we went upstairs. "I can't believe how huge it is! It's like a mansion! You're soooo lucky!"

I felt even more smug, and I think that's when I first started liking her a little. I stopped being Princesscular and started being a Tour Guide instead.

"Below you, on your left, the ballroom, where the grand piano is kept. To your right, as we turn the corner, you will see the Master Bedroom, where Mother sleeps. Opposite is the smaller guest bathroom; the suite is mint with silver trim."

She laughed and laughed. Huh! I got a little upset.

"You're so funny, you know," she said when we got to my room. "I wish I could make people laugh. I can't act comedy at all, I bet you'd be great at it though."

I stopped being upset and beamed at her.

"But you were really good in that play," I said, Graciously and Kindly.

She looked embarrassed.

"I've just had a lot of practice. I went to the Dramarama summer camp last year." She paused. "Avocado was there, too."

"I didn't know you knew Avocado," I said. My heart sank. Probably Keisha and Avocado were best friends, and they would gossip about me and laugh when Keisha went home. Probably...

"I don't think I do anymore, because she

completely ignored me when I went up and said hello at the press conference."

"She is sooo rude! And mean!" I said angrily.

"I thought she was your friend?"

"No way!!! I've only just met her. I thought she was horrible."

"Yeah, me too!" Keisha grinned. "And she was horrible at the Dramarama camp, too. Actually, she nearly got thrown out, because she just spent all her time having tantrums and being mean to people. Like, she only wants to know people if they're really glamorous. Someone told me everyone at St. Agnes' is like that."

Dear Diary, I REALLY liked Keisha then. And it just got better. I couldn't believe how impressed she was with my room, and my walk-in closets. I had been so fed up of only having seven colors to wear, but Keisha made me feel as if I'd gotten a brand new room and a brand new closet. She bounced around like she was in Hollywood or something.

"Oh, wow, your bed has roses on it! I can't believe you have seven closets! Is this your dollhouse? It's amazing! I love it! You are so incredibly incredibly lucky!!!"

Natasha always tells me I'm really lucky because Mother buys me so many things, but there's sort of a limit to how much fun it can be having a disco ball and three TVs and a desk shaped like a fairy-princess sleigh if there's only you to use them. You can even get bored with walk-in closets. But Keisha being so excited made my whole room and all my things seem really cool again. All of a sudden, I did feel lucky.

Then she saw the photo of Poppy and Pepper, my two ponies.

"Are those your ponies? I would so love to be able to ride," she said sadly.

"I hardly ever get to see them," I said.

"Mother's always too busy now to drive me to the stables. Hey, at least you can rollerblade. That's cool!"

She shrugged.

"I suppose so. I'll teach you sometime. It's not hard."

Wow!

Dear Diary, I like Keisha so much!!

This is totally unexpected!!!

I do not know what to do!!!! It is really, really worrying!!!!!

You see, if she was my friend she would come over all the time and things would be fabulous, but, dear Diary, how do I get her to be my friend?

I have the most boring life ever. She will never want to spend time with me when she could be whizzing around on rollerblades with her millions of friends from Clotborough School, being Junior Reporter of the Year.

So this is why I am locked in the bathroom (again! Why is the bathroom the only place you can be private?) while Keisha tries on my hot pink mink and my ecru tutu.

What am I going to do? I've just GOT to impress her!!!! I can't let her see how rotten my life really is!!!!!

Panic, panic, panic, panic, panic, panic!!!!!!!!

Later.

Augh, dear Diary, what have I done??????????
I HATE myself!!!
I've ruined everything!!!!!
Everything is dreadful and it is all, all, all my own fault!!!!!!!!!!!!!!!
GGGGNNNNNAAAAAAAGGGGGGHHHHH
(I don't know what that means, but it is how I feel.)

Oh oh oh oh oh oh oh oh oh oh.

I tried so hard!!!

And then I spoiled it all!!!! I just deserve to be totally this miserable forever and ever. AUGH!!!!

When I came out of the bathroom I had decided I was going to make Keisha like me completely before she left. And I knew I was going to have to do it with my amazing house and my cool stuff, because I don't have anything else. I am not amazing and wonderfully talented like Keisha.

I dragged her away from the closet.

"No time for that now, I have to show you more of my house!" I told her. "I am so completely happy that I just don't need schools, or friends, and who wants to save the world anyway? Not me! Huh!"

I showed her my silver BMX bike and my aquarium, and my real ballet dancer's costume and our swimming pool with my logo on the bottom. I got changed into my swimsuit and did ten lengths without stopping.

"I am a FABULOUS swimmer!" I told her as I got out. I *think* she looked impressed, or maybe just confused. It was a little hard to tell now. Anyway, I was not going to miss a single chance to completely win her over and make her want to be my friend. I showed her the billiard room, and the underground garage, with Mother's Jaguar, and finally the ballroom with the grand piano. I played *Für Elise* twenty-seven times without stopping, really quickly. "I am a FABULOUS piano player," I told her.

I tired myself out with being amazing, but Keisha was definitely looking impressed. Or maybe, now I think of it, just exhausted. Then I thought I had better start giving her things, so she would be grateful as well and so even more likely to be my friend.

"Here! Have a T-shirt! I've got so many I don't need this one!!" I told her.

"*Bathsheba – The Best by Far!*" she read aloud. "Bathsheba, can't we—"

"And have these ecru shoes! They don't really fit me anyway, and they're nicer than yours, obviously, because all my stuff is AMAZING. Come on! We should go and see my huge television and all my game consoles." I bounded down the stairs, but she grabbed my arm.

"Bath! I don't want your shoes! Can we just sit down and talk for a minute?"

"It's Bathsheba, not Bath," I said rather irritably, "and I *am* talking."

"I mean BOTH of us talk, *Bathsheba*. You could let me get a word in edgeways. My mother should be coming to pick me up soon, and we haven't really talked." She sat down on the stairs by the front door.

"My mother's amazing, isn't she?" I said hopefully.

"She's a little...scary."

"That's just because she's so glamorous."

"I like your father better," said Keisha. "*He* calls you Bath."

And, dear Diary, this is when I did the terrible, terrible thing that I will never forgive myself for as long as I live.

It just flashed right into my mind about Bill being a CROOK. And I thought: *Who on earth would ever want to be friends with the daughter of a CROOK?* After all, what if fraud gets passed on? Keisha would never, never want to be friends with a Mini Fraudster (me).

"He's not my father!" I said.
(AUGH!!!)

"Isn't he? He acted like your father."

"Well, he's not," I said desperately. "He's... a distant uncle! So distant he's practically not related AT ALL."

Keisha looked as if she was going to say something else, but then the doorbell rang. We were right next to the front door, so I just got up and opened it.

There stood Bev...and Bill!

"Hello, chick!" said Bill. "How was your day?"

And he tousled my hair in the most horribly Dad-like way.

"Excuse me," said Keisha, very coldly and sternly, and suddenly she looked just like she had the first time I saw her, on the stage at the school play. "Are you Bathsheba's father?"

"Course I am," said Bill cheerfully. "Can't you see? She's got my stunning looks... What's wrong, Keisha?"

Keisha looked at me as if I was a piece of garbage.

"You should feel *lucky*," she said. "My dad died last year." She turned to Bev. "Come on, let's go."

AUGH!!

Just as she was going out of the door – and Bill and Bev were looking totally confused and worried, because they had no idea what was going on – she turned around and said, "You know what, when you came and saw that play, you said I ought to be jealous of you. Well, I am. But not of your stupid swimming pool or clothes, or anything. I just wish I still had a dad."

And then she slammed the door behind her. AUGH!!!!!!!!!!!!!!!!!!!!!!!!!!!

And Bill looked really worried, and said "Bath, what went wrong?"

AUGH!!!!!!!!!!!!!!!!!!!!!!!!!!!!!!!!!

Dear Diary, I just flung my arms around him and went:

"WAAAAAAAAAAHHHHHHH!!!!!!!"

(WHY did nobody tell me her dad died? WHY did I have to be so awful to Bill? WHY am I such a total, complete IDIOT??????????)

I told Bill what I had done. I couldn't help

it. I felt SOOOOOOOO guilty. (I still do.)

Thankfully I did not see the look on his face because I was too busy crying into his shirt. I kept expecting him to push me away, but he didn't. He didn't say anything for a while, and then he said, in a sort of careful-not-to-break-anything voice:

"I see. Well, that is pretty awful."

I just clung on and cried some more.

"Never mind!" he said. "I'll tell you what, I'll drive you over tomorrow and you can apologize."

"But I don't know where she lives!"

"I do. We'll go tomorrow morning. Okay?"

"Okay," I snuffled.

He gave me a hug, and helped me dry my face, and then I just rushed off upstairs to hate myself in peace.

Dear Diary, I am so, so miserable.

I have ruined my whole life even more than it was before.

But I do not really know what else I could have done (I mean before the part about Bill, which I know I should never have done because it was horrible). I just wanted Keisha to like me. How else are you supposed to make friends?

When we told Mother we were going to see Keisha (we didn't tell her what happened, obviously) she dropped her notebook, and said, "What? To that awful place? Bill, I don't think that's very responsible of you!"

And Bill laughed and said "Don't be silly, Amanda, it's perfectly safe. I grew up there, I should know."

And then they had an argument; it was weird, dear Diary, it was like being a real family or something.

Anyway, I will probably be mugged or stabbed and it will serve me right.

Alas, dear Diary, and crud, crud, crud!!!

o o o o o o o o o

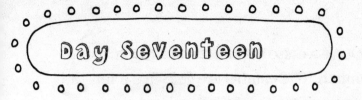

It took about half an hour to get to Keisha's house. I looked out of the bus window and noticed that there were less cafés and more pubs around as we went along. And people did not keep their yards so neatly like Mother said. And there were groups of boys in hoodies lounging (not the same as Reclining) by bus stops. I started getting a little worried, but Bill didn't seem bothered at all. And then I kept thinking about how awful it was going to be seeing Keisha, and I really just wanted to go home.

"Do you think we ought to be doing this?" I asked him. "Mother says it's really dangerous in Clotborough Estates. Maybe we should just go and get chips instead."

He laughed.

"Don't worry, Bath. Your mother stresses too much. The estates are fine. It's a lot better than it was when I was growing up there."

This cheered me up a little. Plus I thought, maybe, as he is an ex-crook, he knows how to deal with the Criminal Element, which is what Mother says lives in Clotborough Estates.

It sort of came into my head, as I was staring out of the window, that Bill could just have said that he never wanted to see me again, when he heard what I said about him.

I mean, it was a terrible thing to do.

I never wanted to see myself again, to be quite honest.

But he stayed.

He didn't go anywhere.

That was Dad-like of him.

Also, there was the time he tried to educate me unexpectedly, by taking me to the Natural History Museum, which from all I have heard is very Dad-like: they stealthily pretend it is all just fun and all of a sudden you find you know what an ichthyosaur is.

I snuck a little glance at Bill, with his bald head and his grubby shoes and his saggy sweater, and I sort of experimented with thinking: *That's my dad.* It felt nice. Strange, but nice.

(And then I thought: *I've totally got to get him some new clothes when I go to America.*)

Even though Mother said such awful things about it, when we actually got to Clotborough Estates I thought it looked okay. There were trees, and a long mural with mirrors in it, and a playground, and lots of green grass. And there were tall apartment buildings rising out of it. They had names painted up their sides: *Burton Tower*, *Taylor Tower* and *Guinness Tower*.

"Keisha lives on the twentieth floor," said

Bill, pointing to Taylor Tower.

I kept very close to him and looked nervously around for muggers as we went into Taylor Tower. A group of boys followed us into the elevator, talking loudly, and one of them was smoking a cigarette, even though he didn't look much older than me. I hid behind Bill. When the boy with the cigarette bumped into me, I was just going to scream, but he said, "'Scuse me," and moved up a little. Huh, so not that scary after all!

When we finally got to the twentieth floor, though, I felt as if my stomach was still way behind on the ground floor. I kept imagining how much Keisha hated me, and I just wanted to turn around and run away.

"It'll be okay," said Bill. "Just be yourself."

"But I don't know how to!"

"Of course you do! Just tell her how you feel."

I gulped. AUGH!!!

Dear Diary,

I thought Keisha would have told her
mother everything, but she couldn't have
because when Bev opened the door she was
completely happy and pleased to see us. She
took us into the kitchen and made Bill tea,
and offered me a cookie, but I couldn't eat
anything because my stomach was jumping
around like a frog.

Keisha wasn't pleased to see us, though.
When Bev called her she came running, but
when she saw it was me she stopped dead and
said, "Oh. It's you."

"Bath wants to have a word with you," said
Bill. "Off you go, Bath!"

I trudged off miserably after Keisha. She
didn't wait for me, but it was not exactly hard to
find her as the apartment is completely tiny. It
does have an absolutely amazing view, though.

Keisha was sitting on her bed with her
arms folded.

"Well?" she said. "What do you want?"

I looked at her room. I couldn't believe how many trophies and certificates and prizes there were everywhere. For rollerblading and acting and reporting, and all kinds of other things like darts and tennis and making the best carnival float. *Wow*, I thought, *she's really modest! She didn't say anything about all this stuff!*

Keisha saw me looking around and turned red.

"Did you just come to laugh at me because I live in a tiny apartment and I don't have a swimming pool? Well, fine, now you can go home!"

"No!" I said, really shocked. "I came to say sorry."

She stared at me.

"I was just getting to like you, and then you went all show-offy and horrible!" she said furiously. "Why?"

I felt so totally miserable. She was obviously going to hate me forever. There was no point in trying to impress her anymore. I might as well just give up. So I did.

"Look," I said, "my life isn't amazing, okay? It's awful! I don't have any friends and I'm totally boring and lonely and miserable. The Bathsheba in the books gets everything right and is so perfect and amazing, and I just wanted to be like her so you would like me."

I didn't know what else to say, so I stopped, feeling hopeless.

Keisha wasn't looking quite so furious, but she wasn't looking happy, either. I glanced around the room. Right in the middle of all the trophies was a photograph in a silver frame. A tall, thin, smiley man, with curly black hair like Keisha, wearing the brightest shirt I'd ever seen in my life. I stared at it. So that's why she was so good at acting A Little Princess.

"I'm really, really sorry about your dad," I said miserably. "I shouldn't have said that about Bill. I felt awful as soon as I said it." I paused. "I said sorry to Bill too. Look, I just wanted you to know I was sorry, that's all. I'll go now."

I was nearly out of the door when Keisha said, "No, wait."

I turned around. She was smiling a little.

"All right," she said. "Apology accepted."

My heart did a double backflip somersault.

"And I don't see why you would want to be like Bathsheba in the books anyway," she added.

"She's perfect," I said, rather shocked.

"No she's not! I know lots of my friends are into the books, but, well, no offense, but I think Bathsheba in the books is kind of a smug, stuck-up snob."

!!

"You're not, though," she said, hastily.

"You're just nice, and friendly, even if you do stupid things sometimes. I mean, like stalking Aunty Tash dressed in a feather boa, that was really funny. I bet the book Bathsheba would never do something like that. I couldn't be friends with her." She paused. "I could be friends with you, though."

Dear Diary, we stayed for about two hours.

Bill and Bev walked over to look at some houses that were for rent not far away, and me and Keisha went along with them, and on the way Keisha showed me how to rollerblade. (This is a LOT more difficult than it looks. It was a good thing there was so much grass and stuff to fall onto.)

On the way we met loads of people who Keisha and her mother said hello to, and they were all really friendly.

Keisha told me all about the drama club at Clotborough School.

"I wish I could join," I said. "It's not much fun doing a play with just one of you."

"You ought to ask your mother if you can go to school. Then you could get into a club. It's so much fun."

"I might ask Mother," I said, totally forgetting I was going to America. "And, ooh, you know what, why don't you come to the stables with me next time we go? I could teach you to ride."

Keisha turned all pink and delighted.

"Wow, *really*? Thanks!"

When Bill finally said it was time to go, Keisha wrote down her phone number for me.

My first ever friend's phone number!

And everything would be so cool – if I wasn't going to America.

I'm in a funny mood, dear Diary. There are not many exclamation marks left in me at the moment.

I have a new friend, which is fabulicious,

but I have to go to America and leave her behind, which is crud.

But I ought to want to go to America, because it will be Glam.

I cannot decide whether my life is ruined or not.

I bet nobody else in all of London has as much to worry about as I do. Natasha always says that if you have a problem you should sleep on it. So that is what I'm going to do, dear Diary. Good night. I am going to bed.

O   O   O   O   O   O   O   O

Day Eighteen

Dear Diary,

I have made up my mind, my life is definitely, one hundred percent, completely and totally ruined!!!

I definitely do not want to go to America!!

In fact I wish Christopher Columbus had just stayed at home and never discovered the stupid place at all, ever!

I cannot think why I wanted to go there in the first place!!

It's like this, dear Diary.

This morning, Mother called me downstairs and into her study.

"Bathsheba," she said excitedly, "I have some news for you – don't touch that, your hands are filthy. Is that ink on your face?"

I shook my head, and then nodded, because I was a little confused by the sentence.

"Bathsheba, darling, I had a wonderful idea!" said Mother. "How would you like to go to school?"

I stared at her.

"I've found the most wonderful one. It's specially for aspiring actresses, and it's just down the road from the villa I've rented in Hollywood. It's called St. Agnes'—"

AUGH!!!

"I'm not going!" I said.

"What?" said Mother. "But I thought it would be ideal. It's exactly like St. Barnaby's. I mean, Avocado goes there! You could even board, if you wanted, and just come home on weekends – that might be convenient, as I will have a very busy schedule—"

"I'm NOT GOING!" I said.

"Bathsheba, I just do not understand you!

You want to come to America, don't you?"

All kinds of ideas went through my head then, dear Diary. It was like when people fall off bridges or something and their Life Flashes Before Their Eyes. It's hard to describe, but it went something like this: AUGH!!!

To get a father (almost a dad) and then suddenly have him whisked away JUST as I was getting used to him!!!!

To find the first possible friend I ever had in all my LIFE and have her whisked away when we were going to do all kinds of things like write articles together and go riding and share clothes and EVERYTHING!!!!!

And they don't have chips in America!!!!!
They only have fries!!!!!!

"No!" I said. "I DON'T want to go to America!!!"

"Then what on earth *do* you want to do?"

We stared at each other angrily. It was

horrible. I've never argued with Mother before. Actually, to be completely exact I didn't really argue with her now, because I just turned around and ran out of the room and ran upstairs to YOU, dear Diary, my one true friend.

Except for Keisha. And possibly Bill.

Who I will have to leave behind to go to America!!!

WAAAAAAAAHHHHHH!!!!!!!!!!!!!!!!!!!

Later.

Dear Diary,

WELL.

I have got a HARD CHOICE to make.

I have never been faced with a decision like this before.

Gosh, I will never complain that I don't know what to wear again.

Now I know what True Responsibility is. After I ran upstairs, I called Bill. I just didn't know what else to do.

"Bill, Mother is going to send me to a boarding school in Hollywood called St. Agnes'!"

"That's where that actress goes, isn't it?" said Bill. "Avocado Dip or whatever her name is. Well…it's certainly very glamorous."

I could tell from his voice he was just trying to be pleased because he thought I wanted to go.

"But Bill, I don't want to go," I said. "I don't even want to go to America!"

"You don't?" he said, sounding much happier, but as if he couldn't quite believe me.

"No. I want to stay here with Keisha!" I paused. "And you."

"Oh, Bath! But what about your mother?" said Bill, sounding completely delighted. "You can't want to leave her?"

"But honestly, she's always so busy. I don't think she'll miss me."

There was a complicated pause. I could sort of hear him thinking very hard on the other end of the phone line. Then he said: "I think I've got a solution. Hang on. I'm coming over!"

When Bill got here, he gave me a big hug, and said, "Don't worry, chick." Then we waited outside Mother's study, as I expect one does outside a principal's office, for her to finish her phone call. She was pretty surprised when we knocked.

"Bill? What are you doing here?" she said.

"Well, Bath called me," he said. "It seems she doesn't want to go to America."

"So she tells me," said Mother irritably. "I suppose I will have to look for a boarding school in England, and that will be even more expensive..."

"No, don't do that," said Bill, "because I've got a suggestion."

He turned to me, and coughed, and said nervously: "I wasn't going to suggest this so soon, but, well, how would you like to come and live with me while your mother's in America?"

My mouth sort of fell open.

"I'm renting an apartment in Clotborough," he said quickly, "but I hope I'm going to get a two-bedroom house soon. It's close to where Keisha and Bev live. Not in the edition, though, Amanda! You could go to Clotborough School, Bath. I hear it's got a good reputation, especially for drama."

I stared at him in amazement. He looked as nervous as I'd felt when I was going to apologize to Keisha. My head went around and around and around, and then around some more. Live with *Bill*?

What if I don't like him?

What if he doesn't like me?

But...Clotborough School! Keisha! Dramarama camp! Rollerblading!

And...no Avocado!

"Bathsheba?" said Mother, staring at me. "You can't honestly tell me you would prefer...living in a tiny house and going to...some ordinary school...to going to St. Agnes'?"

She looked really upset.

"It sounds fun," I said squeakily.

"But Bathsheba...!"

Mother sank back in her chair as if she had been deflated.

"I just don't understand you," she said, but not angrily like before, more as if she had just found out that she really, really didn't, like she realized she had forgotten how to read or something, and then when she opened a book suddenly nothing made sense that ought to.

I felt really sorry for her then. I leaned over

and gave her a hug. She didn't hug me back, but she didn't tell me my hands were dirty, either.

"You don't have to make up your mind right now," said Bill quickly. "Just think about it. There's plenty of time to decide."

SO!!!

Dear Diary!!!!!

I have to choose between being completely glamorous in America with Mother, but being stuck with horrible Avocado and her friends... Or being completely not glamorous in Clotborough. (But maybe going to Dramarama camp! And learning to rollerblade!) And being with Bill, my dad.

I have been trying to think what to do for hours now, and I just am not sure at all.

I thought about looking in my books to get some ideas, but then I decided not to, because after all, they are Fiction. And this is Real Life.

Dear Diary, I really need another person to talk to, a friend, someone who can listen.

But there is only you, and though you are great, dear Diary, you are just paper and cannot give me advice.

CRUD. I wish there was someone else I could talk to. I cannot decide this all by myself!!!!

...Hang on!

I have Keisha's phone number!!!

I wonder if I could talk to her. I wonder if she would listen, or if she would get bored halfway through, or laugh. Or not care.

I suppose I will only find out if I call her.

Back in a minute, dear Diary. Or maybe several minutes.

Three hours later.   ✳

WELL.

I am sooo glad I called Keisha!

She did not laugh, or get bored, or not get it, no, she totally got it and she listened really well and asked sensible questions, and was sympathetic, and loads of help.

She said that if I came to live near her we could go rollerblading every day. And she reminded me that I could join the drama club if I went to Clotborough School (and she says it's a totally fabulous school, and she loves it). And she said we could go to Dramarama camp together.

"Huh, if I even get in," I said.

"You totally will!" she said. "I'm sure you're a really good actress!"

Blush blush blush blush blush, dear Diary!!!

And then she said, "If you wanted to, *you* could write the article for the *Clotborough School Gazette*. All about what it's really like being you, because I bet people would be really interested to know what the *real*

Bathsheba's like, not the book one. I'd help you. You could call it 'Being Bathsheba'!"

Being Bathsheba!
Wow!!!
Like a Star's Autobiography!!!!!

Ooh, dear Diary, I am not sure…
It is a BIG decision…
But I THINK I might be moving to Clotborough!!!!!!!!!!

My Top Ten Favorite Things

Dear Diary,

It feels like I have discovered a LOT of new things since I first took you off the shelf at Paperflo's. Let me tell you about my favorites...

10) Chips and beans! They are now my favorite food. Although Bill says it's probably not healthy to have them every day.

9) Being on the top deck of a bus. SO much more fun than a limousine where you can't see anything from the windows.

8) The Natural History Museum, and seeing the dinosaur that is the size of a bus. Hmm, I wonder what the view is like from the top deck of a dinosaur?

7) Rollerblading... Falling over – getting up – falling over – getting up... It's more fun than it sounds, honestly.

6) Having a friend. A real one!! (No offense, dear Diary.)

5) Having two ponies is still good, especially now I have someone to go riding with (my friend Keisha!)

4) Acting is also still one of my favorite things. The other day Natasha told me I was too theatrical. I said, "Natasha, it is IMPOSSIBLE to be too theatrical, so there!"

3) Stickers. Especially glittery ones. When I go to school (for the first time ever!) I am going to put glittery stickers all over my folders and books and bag, so everyone will see me coming. Ooo, I can't wait!!

2) Keisha's amazing view! Having a house with three living rooms is really cool, of course, but when I look out of Keisha's window, it feels as if her bedroom is as big as the whole sky.

1) Having a Dad. Sometimes having Bill around makes my heart feel as big as the whole sky too.

About the author ♡ ✳

☆

Like Bathsheba's mother, Mandy de Trop, Leila Rasheed is a writer. Unlike Mandy, Leila lives in Birmingham, England. This is not as glamorous as Kensington in London, but it does have a suburb called Hollywood!

Here are some more differences between Mandy and Leila:

☆ Mandy has a diamond-encrusted swimming pool to splash around in.

☆ Leila just has a bathtub to splash around in, which is lucky, as she loves bubble-baths (and Bathsheba!).

☆ Mandy rides around in swishy, dishy limousines.

☆ Leila rides around on buses and trains. She loves walking too — you can explore a lot more on foot than from behind the tinted windows of a limo.

☆ Mandy has a housekeeper to clean up after her.

☆ Leila lives with a saxophonist, who sometimes cleans up, but mostly makes weird and wonderful music.

☆ Mandy writes in a perfectly white office, where nobody is allowed to touch anything in case it gets dirty.

☆ Leila writes in a jumble of computer cables, cookie crumbs and half-empty mugs of tea.

☆ Mandy is often to be found surrounded by fans pleading for her autograph.

☆ Leila is often to be found surrounded by notebooks full of scribbled ideas for new stories, silently pleading to be written.

Find out what
Bathsheba
Clarice de Trop
does next...

The first day of school is never easy...
especially if you've got a celeb reputation
to live up to...

What will Bathsheba do when she goes to
school for the first time in her life?

**Join Bathsheba for her
super-starry second diary!**

OUT NOW!

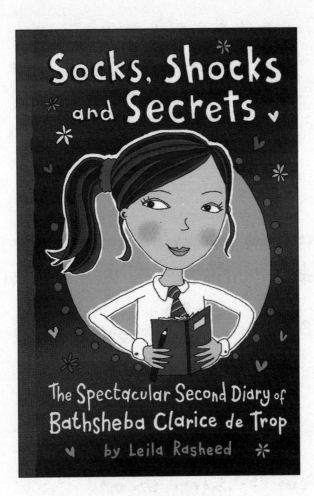

Socks, Shocks and Secrets

The Spectacular Second Diary of
Bathsheba Clarice de Trop

by Leila Rasheed

NEWSFLASH!
Fame and fortune
beckon for
Bathsheba...

Bathsheba finds new friends, an old enemy, and lots of excitement at Dramarama Camp.

But will she REALLY be good enough to appear on Dramarama Diaries?

Find out in Bathsheba's thrilling third diary!

OUT NOW!

Doughnuts,
Dreams and
Drama Queens

The Theatrical Third Diary of
Bathsheba Clarice de Trop

by Leila Rasheed

"An absolute must for any 9⊹ wannabe film stars."
Lovereading4kids.co.uk

What her fans think about Bathsheba's fantastic diary!

"*Chips, Beans and Limousines* is a brilliant and imaginative book. It made me laugh out loud but it also made me think. It is a 5* read, I loved it!!!!!!"
Jessica

"I love this book and I would definitely recommend it."
Kirsty

"A fun read – loved it from the first page!!"
Megan

"After I read this book I knew just what to write my 'Favorite Book Report' on."
Mabel

To the great readers and writers at Writewords

First published in the UK in 2008 by Usborne Publishing Ltd., Usborne House,
83-85 Saffron Hill, London EC1N 8RT, England. www.usborne.com

Inside illustrations by Vicky Arrowsmith.

The name Usborne and the devices ♀ 🌐 are Trade Marks of Usborne Publishing Ltd.

A CIP catalogue record for this book is available from the British Library.

UK ISBN 9780746090916 First published in America in 2011 AE.
American ISBN 9780794530280

JF AMJJASOND/11 00180/2

Printed in Reading, Berkshire, UK.